ANNA SAYBURN LANE

The Crimson Thread

CHAPTER ONE

Alice Delamare hurried through the cloisters. Gusts of wind blew rain sideways past the fluted columns, pattering onto the worn stone flags of the covered walkway. For once, the peace of the old cathedral failed to calm her fears.

The request for a meeting had been unexpected and unwelcome. She checked her wristwatch. In two hours' time, the curtain would go up at the Marlowe Theatre. She had concerns about the play. But she didn't want to miss the start, or to leave William waiting with the tickets.

A tall black-cassocked figure bustled towards her, a bunch of keys clinking in his hands.

'We're closing to visitors now…' He broke off with a smile. 'Oh, I'm sorry, Alice. I didn't realise it was you.'

She smiled back, a little out of breath. She didn't walk so well, these days, and her arthritis was worse when the weather was wet.

'Hello, Derek. Is the Chapter House still unlocked? I just need to…' She trailed off. She'd been warned to go alone. No sense in involving anyone else.

'It is.' The man waited, curious, but Alice said no more.

'Actually, I'm glad I ran into you. Can you spare a minute?'

1

he asked. He looked troubled, slightly furtive.

Alice sighed. She didn't have time to chat. 'Sorry, not really. I'm off to the theatre later,' she said. 'Can it wait?'

'Of course. Another time.' He wished her a good evening.

She pushed through the heavy door and walked into the Chapter House with its high oak ceiling. A little daylight still filtered through the stained glass of the west window, dropping jewels of ruby and sapphire onto the floor. Her fingers went to the silver locket she wore on a chain around her neck, its smooth touch reassuring.

Alice paused before the Prior's Throne and felt in her skirt pocket for the letter.

'It is time for us to talk,' it read. 'We should not be enemies, Mrs Delamare. We serve a common goal. We have much to gain from working together.'

Alice rather doubted that. But she was troubled enough to obey the summons.

'You think it is finished, that Saint Thomas rests safely. You are wrong. The threat is greater than ever. Let us meet in the House of God to resolve our differences.'

The Chapter House was an apt choice, Alice supposed. For hundreds of years, the monks of Canterbury had gathered in this lofty chamber to read a chapter of the gospel and talk through the business of the day. The room must have seen thousands of disputes, resolved one way or another.

Or another. She thought with unease of the other door from the cloisters, which led into the cathedral itself. To the site of the martyrdom, where the dispute between Archbishop Thomas Becket and King Henry II had been settled in bloody fashion, the king's knights murdering the archbishop in his own cathedral. She began to wonder if she should have told somebody – William, at least – about the meeting.

The door slammed shut behind her. She jumped, turned quickly. Not quickly enough; an arm went around her neck and a hand clamped firmly over her mouth.

'Hush,' said a man's voice, right by her ear.

The man's strength made it impossible to struggle; it would be like fighting a block of concrete. Alice couldn't see him properly, but he gave an impression of great bulk.

He marched her to the back of the Chapter House, to the door that was usually kept locked. Holding her with one beefy arm, he turned the handle. It opened onto the back of the cloister, where the library and the side of the cathedral formed a dark corner. Alice tried to shout for help. The arm around her neck squeezed tighter.

'Shut it,' he said. His voice was rough, the accent local. He moved her through the cloister, keeping well into the shadows, and up the dean's stairs into the cathedral. Bewildered, Alice let herself be led. She could hear the sounds of Evensong echoing from the nave. What on earth was he doing?

At the top of the stairs, he turned left, away from the nave, towards a partition in rough-hewn pine which separated the old Water Tower from the rest of the cathedral. He pushed open a door and thrust her through into a short corridor.

At the end, he opened a second door and shoved her through. She staggered and crashed painfully to her knees on the stone floor.

He slammed the door shut, and she heard a padlock being fixed.

'No!' she shouted, banging her hands on the door. She realised she could no longer hear the choristers. Which meant they would not be able to hear her. 'Let me out!' She hauled herself to her feet, her joints protesting.

'Hello, Alice. Sorry, I thought it would just be me.'

Slowly, she turned around. Sitting miserably on the floor in a grey wool suit was her friend and neighbour, William Danbury.

'What… what happened to you?' She sat beside him. Leaning back against the wall, she shivered in her damp clothes, the cold striking up from the flagstones.

'The same as you, I imagine. I'd been asked to attend a meeting, at four o'clock. On my way, I was accosted by that rather unpleasant man and dragged here.'

'My God, William. What's happening? Who is he?'

He reached out and took her hand.

'I don't know. But never fear. We'll get through this,' he said. His voice was brusque, by which she could tell he was as frightened as she was. His hand, however, was firm, despite his years. She grasped it, comforted by its warmth. William and Alice had lived next to each other in the church alms houses for almost fifteen years, but Alice didn't think she had ever touched him before.

'We will,' she agreed. 'One way or another.'

Or another. She shivered again. She wished she was as confident as she sounded.

CHAPTER TWO

'Dr Oddfellow! How marvellous to meet you. I can't tell you how excited I am about tonight.'

Helen smiled and shook yet another hand. The Marlowe Theatre's foyer was full of people, all talking over each other and getting stuck into the free wine. Local dignitaries, academics specialising in Elizabethan drama, important theatrical investors and Christopher Marlowe enthusiasts, some of whom had flown over from America, New Zealand and Japan.

'Me too. Have you come far?'

Helen angled her head so she could see the woman's badge, pinned to an aggressively pink jacket. She was from the Arts Council – a major funder of the production. The theatre's chief executive hovered, looking anxious, as if Helen might say something so controversial that the council would withdraw its grant.

The foyer was very loud and rather hot, after the cool rain outside. Helen found it almost impossible to concentrate on the small talk and introductions. What she really wanted was to sit in silence, alone in the darkened auditorium, until the play was ready to begin. She loved the moment when the anticipatory murmur of the audience stilled into hush as the house lights dimmed. To feel the audience transform themselves from individuals with their own preoccupations into a single creature, intent on the story unfolding on stage.

But as the person who'd discovered the Christopher Marlowe play to be performed for the first time tonight, Helen was in demand. She'd already been quizzed at length by the chairman of the Marlowe Association, who had his own theories about the play's puzzling closing speech. A professor from Harvard University had invited her to lecture on the discovery at their summer school.

She agreed vigorously with the Arts Council woman's views on increasing access to theatre, especially for school-age children.

'You're absolutely right,' she said. 'When I was a teacher, taking children to see plays at the local theatre was one of the most useful things I did. So much better than reading the text in a classroom, don't you think?' She hoped that would help to secure the theatre's grant for another year or two.

Helen's main concern was the short address she'd been asked to make to the audience before the play began. 'Why me?' she'd asked Henry Gordon, the play's director. Why didn't he do it, or someone from the theatre?

'Because you're the one they want to hear from,' he told her. 'It's your story, darling. Tell them about where you found it, and how it was nearly destroyed. That's what they've come for.' Also, Helen knew, Henry suffered from God-awful stage fright. He was only too happy to hand over the duty.

He was now listening to the Marlowe Association man, a rather glazed look on his face. Henry, a big man with an impressive dark beard, usually dressed in baggy jeans and jumpers. Tonight, he looked uncomfortably constrained in a smart dark suit. He kept pulling at the red bow tie around his neck. Helen smiled in sympathy, then saw him take out his mobile phone and check the screen. He frowned and excused himself.

Henry moved through the throng, which parted on either side of him like the ocean making way for a galleon. His face was serious, although he managed a brief smile for the people wishing him luck.

Helen realised he was heading her way.

'Are you all right, my love? Time to get you into the wings for your cameo,' he said.

'What's up? You look like you've had bad news,' she said.

He shrugged his big shoulders. 'Probably nothing. Apparently, there are a few idiots protesting about the play out the front.'

'Protesting? About what? It hasn't even started yet.'

He shook his head. 'Goodness knows. Maybe they don't like the title. Honestly, don't worry about it. Have you met my assistant director? She'll take you down and get you miked up. I need to stay here a bit longer, do some more glad-handing.'

He introduced her to a cheerful-looking woman in her forties with a microphone headset perched on her mop of ginger curls.

'This is Charlie. She'll sort you out.'

Helen's concern was soon replaced by nerves as Charlie led her down the stairs and backstage. The actors, some of whom she recognised from television dramas, were milling around in austere white robes. A young kid dressed as a novice was warming up at the piano, running through scales with a knife-pure voice that raised the hairs on Helen's neck. She had spent a lot of time talking through the text with Henry, but had not met any of the actors before. She'd declined an invitation to sit in on rehearsals, wanting the thrill of seeing the play staged for the first time without preconceptions about how it would be performed.

Rounding a corner, she found herself smiling shyly at Gregory Hall, the actor playing Archbishop Thomas Becket, the controversial anti-hero of Marlowe's play. She'd seen him perform at Shakespeare's Globe several times and thought him one of the best Shakespearean actors of the day. She had been thrilled when she heard he was to take the role. If anyone could take Marlowe's poetry and bring it to dazzling life, he could.

'Thank you for finding this amazing play,' he said, his intense green eyes glittering. 'Break a leg.'

'You too.' She blushed, and wished she'd been able to think of something more original to say. Even his costume of monk's robe and sandals didn't diminish his attraction. She was glad he'd not felt the need to cut his dark curls into a tonsure.

Charlie shot Helen a quick smile. 'We're all a bit star-struck,' she whispered. 'Isn't he great?'

In the wings, a man in a black T-shirt clipped an amplifier pack to Helen's belt and a microphone to her crisp white shirt. She ran her fingers through her cropped hair and wished she could check her lipstick was still in place.

'Do I look all right?' she asked Charlie.

The woman gave her a reassuring smile. 'You look great. Wait for Henry to say your name, then walk into the spotlight,' she said. 'Try not to move outside of it. You'll be in front of the curtain. When you're done, walk straight back here. I'll take the mike, direct you back outside and you'll have time to get to your seat before the play starts.'

Helen bit her lip. Why had she agreed to this?

'Don't worry. You can't see a thing out there with the spot on you. Just pretend you're talking to me, or Henry. You'll be fine.'

Henry strode out of the wings on the other side of the stage and into the light.

'Welcome to the world premiere of *The True History of the Traitor Thomas Becket*, written by Christopher Marlowe in 1593. Before we begin, I'm delighted to introduce the researcher who discovered the play, Dr Helen Oddfellow of Russell University, to say a few words.'

Legs trembling, Helen walked out into the dark theatre until she was bathed in the spotlight. As Charlie had warned, she couldn't see the audience, although she could hear them rustle and mutter. For a moment, she couldn't remember any of her prepared speech.

Breathe, she told herself. They're here to see the play. And the play wouldn't be happening if it wasn't for you.

'The doors are barred,' she began, keeping her voice low. 'You can hear the knights outside, arguing with your servants. It's getting heated. Swords clatter against shields, iron ringing on iron. You know why they're here. Any minute now, you will have to let them in.

'You think to yourself: this is it. This is how I meet my death. You pray. As a medieval Christian, you are filled with terror of hellfire.'

The audience was still. Helen hoped her breathing wasn't amplified in the theatre the way it sounded in her head. Her ears attuning to the silence, she heard someone move. A latecomer, perhaps, trying to find their seat.

'This, then, is the climax of the life of Thomas Becket. And when the Canterbury playwright Christopher Marlowe wrote his account of that life, this is the moment which drew from him the finest poetry, the rawest emotion. The soliloquy you will hear tonight, as Becket anticipates his death, is a masterpiece. It is one of the last things Marlowe ever wrote. And within weeks of writing these words, Marlowe himself was to die at the point of a dagger.

'What were his final thoughts? We can never know. But we know the words he gave to Becket. Death, and how we bear it. The conundrum that poets have wrestled with since the dawn of literature.'

She paused, hearing with gratification a ripple of applause. Then something else. She tried to see beyond the lights, but could make out only a disturbance, a movement. Someone was approaching the stage, down the side of the auditorium. He was shouting. As he reached the first rows of the stalls, she could hear his words clearly.

'Fraud!' he yelled. 'You're a fraud! And this filthy play is a forgery!'

Confused, Helen shaded her eyes against the spotlight, tried to see what was happening. A man stood directly in front of her, chucking handfuls of leaflets into the audience, who sat frozen in their seats. She looked to the wings, saw Charlie shouting, beckoning her to come off. Something hit her in the chest.

She looked down in disbelief. Her white shirt was drenched with crimson.

CHAPTER THREE

The theatre was suddenly full of noise. People were shouting at each other, over shrieks of fear, to get down. The house lights came up on a scene of chaos. Half of the audience members were jumping from their seats, climbing over each other and heading for the exits. A teenage usher tried to calm them, then gave up and fled.

'Ladies and gentlemen…' An announcement boomed over the loudspeaker system, then was abruptly cut off.

Alone on the stage, Helen felt numb. The noise sounded as if it was coming from a long way away. She put a hand to her sodden shirt, sticky with blood, and felt cautiously for the wound. Nothing seemed to hurt, but maybe she was in shock. Maybe this was how it felt when you'd been fatally shot. Before you died. Maybe she was dead already, but didn't know it yet.

The screams and yells seemed to be getting further away. Her head buzzed, full of static. She felt cold, started to sway.

Someone charged onto the stage and grabbed her arm.

'Come on! Can you walk?' It was Charlie.

'I… I think so.' Helen still couldn't feel anything.

'Quickly, then. Let's get you out of danger.'

The man was still there, shouting from the auditorium. Security guards were heading down towards him. Helen followed Charlie, stumbling on jelly legs, and collapsed into a plastic chair in the wings.

'Christ, are you OK?' Henry pushed his way through the dark curtains, his big face sweaty above his black beard.

'She's very pale,' Charlie said. 'Helen, where is the blood coming from?'

Helen clutched her chest. She was breathing. She could feel her heart thumping. The blood didn't seem to be getting any worse.

'I think,' she said slowly, 'I think I'm all right. I don't know what happened, but I don't think I'm hurt.'

Charlie crouched before her. 'Can I see?' Gently, she moved Helen's hands away, and touched a finger to the blood. She sniffed it, then let out a gasp of laughter and licked her finger.

'Thank God for that. It's Kensington Gore.'

'What?'

'Fake blood, stage blood. Made with corn syrup. We use it all the time. He must have chucked a squib at you.'

Helen slumped in relief. 'I thought I'd been shot,' she said. 'I thought…'

She stopped. She'd thought she was dead, but she didn't want to talk about that. Her legs were still trembling.

'Horrible,' said Charlie. 'What a nasty shock.'

They could hear yelling from the auditorium. The man was still shouting.

'Cancel this filthy fraud!' he called. 'Let me go. Get your hands off me.'

Charlie looked at Henry. 'Stay with Helen,' she said. 'I'd better see what's happening.'

Henry ran his fingers through his thick hair. 'Bloody hell. What a mess.'

12

The noise from the auditorium quietened as Charlie walked onstage.

'Ladies and gentlemen, please stay in your seats,' she began, her calm voice rising above the clamour. 'As you can see, we have a bit of an incident. But no-one has been hurt, and we want to keep it that way.'

'Could I have a cup of tea?' Helen asked. She felt sick. The sweet smell of the fake blood wasn't helping.

'Of course. Come into the office. I could do with something a bit stronger, to be honest. How about you?'

'Tea,' said Helen, firmly. She sat on the tatty sofa, surrounded by half-empty coffee mugs and piles of scripts. Framed posters of the theatre's past triumphs loomed down at her. Above the desk, the poster for tonight's performance: a monochrome image of a single candle burning in an ornate silver candlestick, wax pooling like blood at its foot.

Henry filled the kettle and set it to boil. The theatre's chief executive, a short man in a slightly too-tight suit, popped his head around the door.

'Ah, Henry. Dr Oddfellow. I hear it was a false alarm. Thank goodness you weren't harmed,' he said.

'No thanks to your security,' said Henry. 'What's happening front of house?'

'Well, the guards got the chap. They think he was with that bunch of protestors I texted you about. There was no way we could have known someone would try to stage a stunt like this.'

Henry raised his eyebrows. 'Really?'

'The police have arrived. They're talking to him.' The man tried a business-as-usual smile. 'Question is, what do we do now?'

The two men stared at each other.

'The show must go on?' asked the chief executive, with a shaky laugh. He really didn't want to have to cancel, Helen realised, what with the Arts Council and all the newspaper critics who'd been enticed down from London.

Henry stood, his face stony. 'I'll talk to the actors,' he said. 'I'm not forcing anyone to perform after that. Not if they don't feel safe.'

'Right.' The man rubbed his hands together. 'Good. I'll leave that to you, then. I'd better go and talk to the sponsors.' He bustled out of the door.

Henry handed Helen the tea. She took a sip and grimaced. 'Sweet.'

'Sorry. I thought you're supposed to put sugar in when someone's had a shock.'

Helen rolled her eyes. 'I think that's just in the movies.'

Charlie put her head around the door. 'How's it going? I've asked the audience to bear with us for fifteen minutes while we assess the situation. The stage is being cleaned.'

'The theatre people want to go ahead,' said Henry. 'But I won't force anyone to go on.'

'You know what actors are like,' said Charlie. 'They won't want to be the ones to cancel. They're all geared up, especially Greg.' She turned to Helen. 'What about you, Helen? You didn't get to finish your speech.'

Helen looked up, startled. 'You mean... I should do it again?' She hadn't even thought about going back out there.

'Only if you want to,' said Henry, hastily. 'And perhaps it would be better to do a quick bit at the end, rather than repeat the whole thing from the start. Assuming we do go ahead, we should aim to get the curtain up as soon as possible.'

'Why don't I talk to the police?' said Charlie. 'See what

14

they advise. Then we can talk to the actors, and make an announcement once we've decided.'

'Right.' Henry was on his feet, looking businesslike. 'Helen, are you all right here for a bit? I'll come with you, Charlie. Then we can get the show on the road.'

Left alone, Helen drank her tea and imagined walking back onto the stage. Fraud, he'd called her. A fraud, with a forged play. A filthy play. She frowned. Only one other person had called it that before. And it couldn't be him.

Fraud. She imagined the audience starting to cat-call, voices joining in around the theatre. Fraud. Fake. Liar. She shivered again, pressed her eyes shut. She wasn't sure she could do it.

The manuscript of the play – what remained of it after the fire – had been authenticated by experts. Her reconstruction of the text, using the damaged manuscript and her partially completed transcript, had been approved by the Russell University Press, which had published the first edition. But some of the work had relied on her memory. There had been times when she'd felt almost like a medium, musing over a half-destroyed line until something – the spirit of Christopher Marlowe, if she'd believed in such things – whispered the missing words into her ear. It wasn't forgery. But it wasn't exactly orthodox academic work, either. She'd always been uncomfortable trying to explain the process to others.

There was a tap on the door. The man from the Marlowe Association hovered.

'Glad to hear you're all right,' he said. 'Given the events – and the previous questions around the play's provenance – I wondered if I might present a few thoughts of my own?'

Without waiting for an answer, he came in.

He hitched up his corduroy trousers and sat on Henry's desk, exposing bony ankles. He pulled out a sheaf of paper.

'I have prepared a short speech on behalf of our association. Regarding the handwriting analysis, the carbon dating of the leather ties, and so on. Something that might address the fears of forgery.'

'What do you mean?' Helen flushed. 'It's not a forgery. You've seen the evidence. It's all in the papers I've published.'

He pressed his fingers together. 'Of course. And perhaps that is the approach we should be taking. I don't suppose you will want to go on stage again, after that unpleasantness. I suggest I address the audience in your place. On behalf of the Marlowe Association, in light of our reputation.'

Helen set down her mug and got to her feet. 'Kind of you, but there's no need. I'm more than capable of speaking to the audience after the play. In fact, I'm looking forward to it.'

'But… I really think…' Pink spots had appeared in his sallow cheeks.

'Please excuse me,' she said. 'I'd better see if the wardrobe department can find me a clean shirt.'

CHAPTER FOUR

J oshua Jones stood in the chilly corridor, one hand tapping the piano keys. Inside the green room (which wasn't really green), the cast was discussing whether or not to go ahead with the opening performance. He was praying hard. It would spoil everything if they cancelled.

He'd been looking forward to it so much: his mum and dad in the audience; his brother and sister sitting alongside them. This was his time to show them what he could do.

'Are you all right, Josh? Do you need a glass of water?' His chaperone, one of the music tutors from school, was fussing again. He shook his head. He wished she would leave him alone.

He just wanted to get out there, now. They'd been practising for ages. He liked the theatre. The actors made a fuss of him, and it felt like being in one big, exciting gang. There were three of them from the cathedral choir, performing on alternate nights in the role of the novice who sings at the start of the play. He'd been so excited to be picked for the opening performance. He didn't think he could stand it if Finlay or Ben got to do it instead.

Josh stopped fiddling with the piano and slipped quietly into the wings. He peeped out through the heavy curtains. They were still there, his family, lined up patiently in the middle of the stalls, practically the only black faces in the whole audience. There to watch Josh, the middle child; to actually sit in silence for once while he sang. He resisted the impulse to wave at his mum or stick his tongue out at Ethan. He was a professional, now.

He didn't see why they were thinking about cancelling the show. After all, the woman who got hit with fake blood wasn't even in it, and she hadn't been killed or anything. The man who'd done it had been grabbed by the security guards and bundled into a store room. Josh had seen the police taking him away afterwards. Disappointingly, he hadn't been in handcuffs. He didn't look very threatening, either. He reminded Josh of his history teacher: a small man with a straggly grey beard and sticking-out teeth. He wasn't saying anything, just looking at the floor. Josh wondered if he'd be sent to prison.

'Josh, where are you?'

He sighed and pushed back through the black curtains to the corridor.

'Don't wander off like that.' The chaperone was looking excited, though, not annoyed.

'What's happening? Are we going on?'

Charlie came out of the green room with a big smile. 'Cheer up, Josh. Ten minutes to curtain. How's that solo sounding?'

'Yes!' The grin almost split his face. He'd been dreading the thought of having to go back to Choir House. All the boys would be waiting to hear how it had gone, and he really didn't want to have to tell them there had been no performance, that everyone had been sent home.

'Come on,' said his chaperone. 'I'll make you some honey and hot water. You need to let your throat relax.'

The white-painted room was bursting with people, the actors in their long robes all looking happy. Josh found a seat in the corner of the tatty blue sofa and sat, cross-legged, sipping his hot water.

'Feeling nervous?' It was Gregory Hall, the actor that his mum said was really famous. His voice was low, so you had to listen hard to hear him. 'Don't worry. You'll be fine.'

Josh wasn't nervous, not now. He wished everyone would stop telling him not to worry. In his experience, that usually meant there was something to worry about.

He worried about real things, like whether his sister was remembering to walk his dog, and whether his mum was all right. Singing was easy. When the music started, it just filled him up, like some sort of gas that made him lighter than air. When the choir sang together, it was as if they all lifted up off the ground, floating above the audience, the different voices like clouds you could bounce on, climb up and roll down. Singing alone was different, but brought that same sense of weightlessness, of soaring upwards. The best thing about being in the choir was that he didn't have to try to explain that. Everyone knew. You didn't feel like a weirdo for needing to sing.

'Come on, Josh. What are you daydreaming about? You're on in three minutes.'

He put down the mug and got up. His chaperone straightened his robe, reminded him to take off his trainers. Barefoot, he walked to the side of the stage, carrying the solo carefully within him like a bowl of soup he didn't want to spill. The actors dressed as monks let him through to the front. Someone handed him the big candle and he walked slowly into the light as the first note of the organ sounded, a droning monotone that gave him all he needed.

'*O vis eternitatis...*' he began, his voice steady and clear, sending the notes out into the auditorium, where his family sat. Oh power in eternity. He led the procession around the stage, trying not to sneeze at the clouds of incense from the actor behind him swinging the thurible. The words unspooled, a golden thread. He stopped at the foot of the big cross that had been erected at the back of the stage, where Gregory Hall stood, and the final notes fell away.

A second's silence. He heard from the audience a smatter of applause, followed by shushing, and wondered if that had been his family. He hoped not. He'd explained to them before that you don't clap at the end of a votive, even if it's really good.

He handed the candle to Gregory Hall, who gave him a quick wink as he took it, his back to the audience.

That was it, his big bit over. He remembered what the director, Henry, had said. Don't get distracted when you've finished the solo, Josh. Keep still, watch Greg and don't slump. Pretend that everything he says is fascinating, even if you've heard it a million times before. Josh had tried to explain that was exactly what the choir had to do in Evensong every night, but Henry hadn't really listened. As if Josh was about to get his phone out and start playing games.

Ten minutes later, he followed the procession back off-stage, last this time, in silence.

'Brilliant, Josh. Well done,' whispered Charlie. He flushed as she squeezed his shoulders tight. 'Back to the green room.'

This was the boring bit. He didn't go back on stage till the end of the play, which left him with two and a half hours of waiting around, to do prep or have a nap. He yawned. He was always knackered after a solo.

Josh pulled his trainers on and looked without enthusiasm at his history workbook, thinking again of the funny little man who'd thrown the fake blood.

'I'm tired,' he told his chaperone. 'Can I go outside? Maybe some fresh air will wake me up.' That was the sort of thing adults said to him, especially on winter mornings when he didn't want to get out of bed.

The woman didn't look keen. 'It's been raining. But I suppose a bit of air won't hurt. I'll get my coat.'

He waited till she'd turned her back, and darted from the room, heading for the stage door.

It was cool outside, still drizzling a bit. It felt good to be on his own. He mooched over to the stone bridge that spanned the River Stour. Streetlights illuminated the streaks of bright green weed that rippled below the surface. He picked up a pebble and dropped it into the water. It disappeared with a satisfying plop. He watched the ripples spread, feeling within himself the ripples of his solo becoming still.

It had been good, he knew that. Walking onto the stage, sending his voice out into the audience – he didn't really want to do anything else. He hadn't dared explain that to his family, yet. They'd been surprised when the minister at their church had said Josh had an exceptional voice and should try out for the cathedral choir. They'd been even more surprised when he'd been accepted. But to do this all his life – assuming he still had a good voice in a year or two, once it had broken – would be something else altogether.

He scuffed along the river path, past the bench with the statue of the man on it, towards the Beerling Hall where the choir had performed a Christmas concert the previous year. The flint building was ancient, they'd been told, one of the old

21

pilgrim hostels. It had been cold and a bit damp inside.

A sound caught his sharp ears and he stopped. Plash, plash, coming from the water. A canoe glided past, a figure in a dark anorak hunched over the paddle, hood up against the drizzle.

The boat disappeared into the darkness under the bridge. Funny time of night to go rowing, Josh thought.

'Joshua! Where are you?' His chaperone, her annoying voice with an edge of desperation. He turned, raised his hand.

'Here.'

He supposed he should go back in. With one last glance at the ripples left by the boat, he retraced his steps to the theatre.

CHAPTER FIVE

William cleared his throat. 'Are you cold? Let me give you my jacket.'

'I'm fine, thank you.' Alice pulled her raincoat tighter around her and wished she'd put on a warmer cardigan.

Rain hissed against the stained glass windows which rose tall above them, saints with red and blue robes topped by heraldic shields. The external floodlighting of the cathedral threw a little light down through the windows, barely enough to see by.

The room was round, with walls of unpainted stone. Alice had been to one or two meetings there, when it had housed a small display about monastic life. The Water Tower had once been used as a lavatorium, where the monks paused to wash their hands in a big stone basin in the centre of the room before entering the cathedral. But the whole of the north-west transept was earmarked for restoration work, and the tower room had been closed for months. No-one would come their way, unless they knew they were here.

Alice wondered how long it would be before their abductor came back.

She brought out the letter. 'Did you get one of these?' she asked.

William nodded and reached inside his suit jacket. They smoothed the letters out and compared them, straining to see in the poor light.

Both letters had been sent through the post in anonymous white envelopes, the postmark local. Both were printed on headed paper and formally addressed. No signature. The letter heading was the same: Father Francis Nash, Christianity in Crisis, Minor Canon Row, Rochester.

But Francis Nash was dead, as Alice and William knew only too well. They'd been the ones to find his body in the church which held the secret they had guarded for so many years.

'I suppose this is about Saint Thomas's resting place.' William always gave Becket his due reverence.

'I suppose so.' Alice sighed. Henry II's turbulent priest continued to cause trouble, eight hundred years after his murder in Canterbury Cathedral.

As far as Alice was aware, the secret of the saint's burial place was now known only by William, herself, and Charles Fairfax, former master of Eastbridge Hospital. And Charles was in Australia, driven to the other side of the world by the tragic events that had led to Father Nash's death. William Danbury had been appointed master in his place.

'Does anyone else know? The letter talks about sharing our knowledge.'

William shook his head. 'No. Except for the researcher who found the play. Miss Oddfellow.'

'Of course.' Helen Oddfellow had unearthed the long-hidden Christopher Marlowe play that clearly signposted the location of the grave, for those with the brains to follow the clues. Helen, not short on brains, had arrived at the little church on the hill, next to the alms houses where William and Alice lived. Alice had been the one to let her in. And that was when the trouble had started up again.

'Do you trust her? I know you've met her from time to time, since it happened.' William's voice was abrupt.

'I do. I like her, William.' Alice had sensed something of a kindred spirit in the restless young woman, her quiet determination to find the truth. 'She wanted to understand. Not to cause trouble. Don't you think?'

He sighed. 'I hope so. I really hope so.'

'Who do you think sent the letters? I thought Christianity in Crisis had been disbanded,' Alice said. The Church of England had been horrified to discover links between Francis Nash's campaigning organisation, with its traditional values agenda, and a violently right-wing English nationalist group which protested against immigration and Islam.

'You can disband a group, but that doesn't mean the people disappear,' said William. 'I suspect there are plenty of them still around. Trouble is, I never gave Francis Nash the time of day, so I don't know any of his hangers-on.'

'Do you think it has something to do with the play?' asked Alice. Both she and William had trusted Helen's promise that the play's epilogue, with its tantalising clues, would not be performed. The two of them had planned to watch the play together, have supper afterwards and share a taxi home. It was a prospect that Alice had been looking forward to for weeks. She had rarely been to the theatre since Mark died.

'It must be. That's what the letter means, doesn't it? "We will not stand by while Saint Thomas is insulted. To defend the church, we must defend Saint Thomas." I mean, it has to be,' said William. He looked uncomfortable. 'Derek Bryce said someone had been in touch with the library, asking if they had what they called the real manuscript of the play. I thought it might be best to move the epilogue.'

'Ah.' Alice remembered Derek's troubled face, earlier that evening in the cloister. That must have been what he wanted to talk to her about.

They fell silent again. Alice felt for her pendant. 'Oh, no.' She ran her fingers around her neck. The fine silver chain was missing.

'What is it?'

'Nothing. It's just – I've lost my pendant. The chain must have broken when the man grabbed me.' She thought with regret of the keepsake within it.

'That's a pity...' he began. Alice caught a faint noise from the corridor.

'Hush,' she said. She strained her ears. 'Listen.'

'Sorry,' whispered William. 'My hearing isn't so good.'

She could hear it more clearly now. Footsteps, coming closer. A chink of keys. The padlock rattled.

Alice clutched William's hand again.

The dark figure in the shadowed doorway was tall and slim, in a long coat.

'My assistant is waiting outside,' said a cultivated voice. A woman's voice. 'He'll come in if I call him. It would be better for you if I don't need to do that.'

William began to get to his feet.

'Sit down, Mr Danbury. Stay there, both of you.'

The woman closed the door with care and walked over until she loomed above them, her silhouette densely black against the windows.

'Let's keep this simple. I want to know where Saint Thomas Becket is buried. Father Nash was on the verge of making

26

that discovery when he was killed. Tell me now, and you will both be found, safe and well, when the cathedral is opened tomorrow morning.'

Alice frowned. She knew that voice, she was sure of it. There was something familiar behind the over-refined tone, as if the woman had had elocution lessons and was always careful to check herself for sloppy pronunciation. Alice peered into the darkness, trying to see the woman's face.

'If you know anything about me at all, you know I won't tell you,' said William, the old soldier, his voice gruff.

'In which case, you will not be found safe and well,' she replied. 'Which may not concern you much, Mr Danbury, but you would be sorry to see Mrs Delamare suffer.'

Alice's hand was almost crushed as William clenched his fist.

'This has nothing to do with Alice,' he said. 'She doesn't know anything about Saint Thomas's grave. Do what you like with me, but you might as well let her go. Waste of your time.'

The woman laughed. Again, that over-cultivated tone, as if someone had once told her to try to laugh like a peal of bells. There was something behind it, Alice thought. An accent, suppressed but familiar.

Come on, she told herself. Who is she?

'Chivalrous,' the woman said. 'But nonsense. You've known for years, haven't you, Alice? You've spent half your life preventing Saint Thomas from being translated back to the cathedral where he belongs.'

Alice said nothing. She had indeed known for years. Her husband had vouchsafed the secret to her decades ago.

Mark Delamare, academic and vicar, had for some years been the master of Eastbridge Hospital, an ancient pilgrim hostel close to the city walls. The secret had been known only to a small circle of people connected to Eastbridge, who kept the martyr's lamp burning and quietly tended the shrine. Its enormous significance in the Tudor and Elizabethan eras had been almost forgotten. And the deeper secret Thomas Becket's grave guarded was protected still.

Alice did not think that this woman was ready for that secret. Or, indeed, that the wider world was ready. Perhaps it would be, one day. Alice hoped she might live to see it. But for now, some secrets were best left undisturbed. The question was, at what cost?

'Haven't you?' The woman leaned closer, a faint waft of perfume triggering Alice's memory. Flowers, she thought. Something to do with flowers. She closed her eyes, trying to remember.

A stinging slap across her cheek, and her head snapped back against the wall.

'Stop it!' shouted William. He started to scramble to his feet again, tried to interpose himself between Alice and the woman.

'Oh, do sit down.' The woman shoved him, caught him off-balance. He fell heavily to the ground, let out a cry.

'William! Be careful.' Alice reached out and took his hand. He gripped her fingers tightly, lying awkwardly on his side.

'I'm all right.' His breath was coming fast.

'What hurts?' she asked.

'Nothing. Just bumped my hip. Won't be a moment.' His voice was taut with pain. Damn, thought Alice. He's broken it. She squeezed his hand.

'Stay still, William. Don't move.' He needed an ambulance. She had to find a way to get him help.

She turned towards the woman. 'You're right,' she said. 'I do know. And I think I know you, too, from somewhere. Why

28

don't you remind me who you are? You know what us old ladies are like. Terrible memories.'

The woman laughed again, that irritating peal of bells. 'Good try, Alice. There's nothing wrong with your memory. Tell me now, and we can get this over with.'

Alice took off her raincoat and folded it under William's head. 'William needs to go to hospital,' she said. 'I'll tell you after the ambulance has taken him away.'

'Oh, I don't think so. But perhaps I might call an ambulance, once you've told me.'

'Why are you doing this now?' Alice asked. 'If, as you say, I've known half my life, why are you suddenly demanding I tell you today? Is it something to do with the Marlowe play?'

'The play,' said the woman, enunciating carefully, 'is a piece of filth. It will be stopped. It disrespects the memory of Saint Thomas.'

Interesting, thought Alice. That was Father Nash's opinion. He had hated the play so much, he attempted to burn the original manuscript, keeping only the epilogue. The manuscript of the epilogue had been in Nash's pocket when they'd found his body. William had removed it before the arrival of the emergency services. Later, he had arranged for it to be hidden away in the cathedral archives, placing it where it was unlikely to be disturbed.

'Have you read it?' she asked. 'Father Nash thought it contained the secret. Maybe you could work it out for yourself. I might even be able to help you.'

William raised his head. 'Don't tell her anything,' he said. 'Keep the faith, Alice. I'll be fine.'

The woman walked silently to his side and contemplated him for a moment, a thin bundle of neatly dressed bones huddled on the floor. Delicately, she placed one shiny black boot on his hip. Then she stamped on him.

His gasp of pain went straight to Alice's heart.

'Stop it! Don't hurt him, please.' Alice hunched over his body, trying to protect him from any further blows.

'Darling?' called the woman.

The door opened and a man walked in. He was huge, Alice realised, at least six foot tall and heavily built. A hooded anorak made it impossible to see his face.

'We are finished with Mr Danbury,' the woman said. 'Take him outside, as we discussed. Alice, I think it's time for a change of scene. We're going to take a short walk. If you want your friend to get to hospital, I suggest you keep very quiet and do as I say.'

'We stay together,' said William, his voice strained. Alice could tell what an effort it was taking him not to cry out in pain. She gripped his hand and quickly dipped her head to kiss his damp forehead. Then the giant was upon them.

Alice was dragged away, shoved backwards until she staggered into the wall. The giant hoisted William into his arms as if he weighed nothing at all.

'Please be careful with him,' said Alice.

If the woman was taking her outside the cathedral, she thought, she could scream for the constables who patrolled the close all night. They'd be there in seconds, ready to rescue her and William.

'I'll get help, William,' she called. 'I promise.'

'Tell her nothing,' he replied. 'Keep the faith.'

The man pushed him through the door into the cathedral.

'How nice,' said the woman, brightly. 'Just you and me.'

CHAPTER SIX

The applause showed no sign of dying down. Helen wiped tears away with her thumb. She stood among the audience, all of them on their feet, cheering as the actors took yet another curtain call.

Gregory Hall stepped forward and signalled for quiet. The audience hushed.

'Thank you all so much,' he said. 'This means a lot to us.'

Helen suddenly remembered what she was supposed to be doing. 'Excuse me,' she whispered to the woman on her right.

'Before we began, you were listening to Dr Helen Oddfellow telling you about the play. As you saw, she was most rudely interrupted. But I'm delighted to say Helen has agreed to say a few words to conclude this extraordinary evening.'

Helen squeezed her way through the audience and up the steps. She walked onto the stage and shook his hand.

'You were brilliant,' she told him, heart full. 'Thank you so much.'

She turned to the audience. The house lights came up. She felt more comfortable now she could see people ranged across the brightly lit auditorium. She realised she'd left her notes in the bag by her seat, but that didn't matter; she knew what she wanted to say.

'Wasn't that amazing?' she asked. The audience cheered in approval. 'When I first held the manuscript of this play in my hands, I knew it would be something special,' she began. 'But a play doesn't live until it's performed. I'm pretty overwhelmed right now. I'm sure you are, too. I could never in a million years have imagined this performance, with its nuance and emotion, its historical authenticity, yet timeless relevance. I'd like to thank the whole company, from the bottom of my heart.'

She took a breath. 'As you heard, the protester who inter-rupted us earlier accused me of forgery. Well, I have one thing to say to him. Do you think, if I could write something as wonderful as this, I would pretend that someone else wrote it?'

Laughter rippled through the auditorium.

'I could tell you about the handwriting analysis, and the carbon dating, and the other tests of authenticity,' she said. 'But you can read all that in the academic papers. I think the true test of authenticity is this – the performance. It radiates truth. As you have seen, the play is entirely of its time, reflecting the uneasy relationship between church and state in the Elizabethan era.

'I am sure that Christopher Marlowe, if his spirit is anywhere today, will be revelling in this performance, in the theatre named for him, in his home town.'

Glancing around the audience, she saw the man from the Marlowe Association, his lips pressed into a thin line. The Arts Council woman was clapping hard, a big grin on her face. Helen's gaze fell on two empty seats in the stalls; the only ones apart from her own that were unoccupied. Who was missing? She scanned the packed house.

Alice Delamare, she realised, from the alms houses at Harbledown. Alice had promised to come. Helen had been

32

looking forward to talking to her afterwards, to see what she made of the way the production had dealt with Marlowe's depiction of Becket as a duplicitous traitor. She'd call Alice tomorrow, find out what had happened.

Helen walked into the wings, where Henry was waiting with two champagne flutes in his hands. She hugged him carefully, trying not to spill the bubbly liquid.

'Here you go, my darling,' he said. 'I think we all deserve one of these.'

Backstage, the actors were jubilant. There was music playing in the green room and people were dancing, drinking champagne from plastic cups, wiping off make-up and removing their ecclesiastical robes to reveal T-shirts and jeans underneath. Henry was quickly mobbed, a group of actors pulling him into a conga-line. Helen laughed and evaded his attempts to take her with him. She took a swig of the champagne, cold and delicious.

She spotted Charlie, who had changed into a sparkly gold top, talking to the small kid who'd played the novice. Charlie waved her over.

'Well done! I loved your speech. And I know it wasn't easy, going on again after the attack.'

'I saw the police take him away,' said the kid. 'Will he go to prison?'

'I doubt it,' said Charlie. 'Helen, have you met Joshua Jones, undoubted star of the show? Josh, this is Helen, who discovered the play.'

'Hi, Josh. You were great. Do you enjoy singing?'

'Hello.' He smiled politely, but his attention was elsewhere. 'There they are!' he shouted, pushing his way through to the open door, where two smartly dressed adults and children stood, looking a little uncertain.

Charlie laughed. 'I guess that must be his family. He's one of the cathedral choristers. They board, so don't get to see family that often.'

'I suppose not. Do you have family here tonight?'

The woman shook her head. 'My dad lives in the States. I'm not close to the rest of the family. How about you?'

'No.' Helen felt a pang of grief for her own father, knowing how much he would have loved the play. 'My parents died years ago, and I don't see my sister much.'

They stood in silence for a moment.

'Families, eh?' said Charlie, reaching for a bottle from the table. 'Top up? How're you doing? You look pooped.'

And suddenly, Helen was exhausted, longing to be away from the noise and the people.

'Yeah, I think I'll head back to the hotel. It's been quite a night.' She put the champagne flute down on a table.

'You sure? There's always a bit of a party after the first night.'

'So I see.' A party was the last thing Helen felt like right now. 'Thanks, but I need some air.'

She weaved her way through the crowd, past the real star of the show holding court in the middle of the room, and out of the door. The corridor was deserted and blissfully quiet.

She heard a brief blast of music as the door opened and closed again.

'Don't go. I wanted to ask you something.' It was Gregory Hall. He leaned against the white breeze-block wall. She could feel the heat coming off him, smell the sharp fresh sweat darkening his grey T-shirt. Without his stage makeup, she could see the violet smudges under his eyes. He looked exhausted. Helen remembered reading that he was renowned

34

for giving everything he had to a performance, then sleeping most of the next day.

'Of course.'

'That final speech. The bit about the Alcoran. He's referring to the Quran, isn't he?'

Helen nodded. She'd been through this with Henry. 'Yes. Marlowe mentions it in other plays, like *Tamburlaine the Great*. He seems to have been quite interested in Islam. The Elizabethan age was a time of exploration, as you know. Finding out about new countries, new religions.'

'Sure. The Elizabethan era. But he's writing about the Middle Ages. Is he really saying that Thomas Becket would have had a copy of the Quran? And that he'd be referring to it in his last moments?'

Helen hesitated. He'd really thought about this, she realised. His eyes held hers, bright with curiosity despite his fatigue. And that final speech made little sense unless you knew what she had learned from Alice Delamare, the secret that Becket had taken to his grave.

'Marlowe was bringing his own interests to bear on the past, as we always do,' she said. 'But the medieval world was wider than we often imagine, you know?'

'Go on. This is interesting,' he said.

'Well, Becket was exiled to Europe for many years,' said Helen. 'He would have met scholars in the monasteries of France, some of whom had travelled to the great centres of learning, Cordoba and Granada in Spain. Remember, this was the time of Al-Andalus. Much of Spain and Portugal was under Muslim rule. And the crusades were still underway, with clashes between Islam and Christianity in Jerusalem. Europe was not purely Christian, nor was it isolated from other religions.'

Gregory steepled his fingers, reminding her for a moment of Richard.

'So he might have seen a copy. But in the play, he refers to it, talks about what it has to say about death. There's more going on, isn't there? What did Marlowe know, Helen?'

She smiled. 'If I knew what Marlowe knew, I could stop researching him tomorrow,' she said. 'It's intriguing, I agree.'

He laughed, showing even white teeth. Hollywood teeth, Helen thought, unkindly.

'I'd love to know more. Because it feels to me as if Marlowe is trying to tell us something, hinting at some big secret. Not just in that final scene, but throughout the play. Do you think you found it all? Or was there a scene missing somewhere, something to explain the Quran reference?'

Helen thought uncomfortably of the epilogue, hidden in the cathedral library, less than a mile away.

'If there was more, I'm afraid it must have been lost in the fire,' she said, hoping she wasn't blushing too badly. She really wasn't good at lying.

'I suppose so. Thanks again, Helen. It was good to meet you.' He clasped her hand and looked into her eyes for a moment longer, a question lingering. 'I'd like to talk more about it. Maybe we could have dinner sometime?'

'That'd be nice,' Helen muttered. She extracted her hand and fled. Had Gregory Hall just asked her out on a date? Don't be ridiculous, she told herself, walking fast through the foyer and out onto the street. He wants to know more about the play. And she'd better not go, or she'd end up telling him more than she should. She didn't think she'd be able to resist that intense gaze for long.

Helen hadn't been on a date since Richard, the historian who first set her on the track of the Marlowe play. She'd resisted all further thoughts of romance. It seemed... not wrong, exactly, but irrelevant. Love was something that happened to other people.

Still, though. Gregory Hall had said they should have dinner. She'd admired him as an actor for years; had never expected to meet him, never mind talk to him. What a night this was turning out to be.

She walked up the narrow street from the theatre, past the Pilgrims Hotel and the Canterbury Tales pub. History was everywhere in Canterbury. She turned left into the High Street, pausing for a second opposite the flint-faced Eastbridge Hospital. It had been within the walls of that ancient foundation that she'd worked out at least some of the secrets hidden in Marlowe's play. And then the rest, Alice Delamare had told her, sitting in the quiet church on the hill.

She'd call Alice in the morning. Maybe she'd had to leave before the end, because of the delayed start. Helen would walk over to Harbledown and have tea in her tiny, peaceful alms house, before taking the train back to London.

She reached the smart hotel where Henry had insisted on putting her up for the night. Her room was big, silent and anonymous, with no distracting history. She cleaned her teeth, undressed and slid into the crisp, cool sheets. She didn't expect to sleep, with so much buzzing around in her head. Minutes later, she was dead to the world.

CHAPTER SEVEN

Helen woke with a jolt. For a second, she didn't know where she was. At home, she slept with the amber glow of streetlights illuminating her bedroom, the constant noise of traffic from the busy road. The silence and darkness of the unfamiliar hotel room felt smothering.

She raised herself on one elbow and reached for the bedside lamp. It cast a soft light across the white sheets and neutral walls. She reached for her phone, saw with dismay that it was barely six o'clock.

She drew back the heavy curtains. It was still dark outside, the pedestrianised High Street empty of people. The room was too hot, but the windows didn't open and she couldn't be bothered to fiddle around with the air conditioning.

It was over. She'd been working towards it so long, the performance of the play she'd unearthed from four centuries of obscurity. And the first night had been an undoubted success, despite the unsettling interruption from the protestor.

Helen felt responsible for the play, as if it really had been her, not Marlowe, who'd written it. She was so relieved it had been well-received. It would become a classic, she thought with wonder, performed by the world's greatest theatre companies. It would enter onto school and university syllabuses, to be pondered over and discussed for years to come.

Her thoughts returned, as always, to Richard. If only he could have been with her to see it. Sitting beside her in the audience, his hand warm on hers. The play had been his discovery, too.

She thought, almost guiltily, of Gregory Hall. Something about his evident intelligence, his astute questioning, had ignited memories of Richard. Her heart gave a quick jump as she remembered his suggestion they have dinner. She told herself again not to be silly.

Hastily, she pulled jeans and a black cashmere sweater from her overnight bag. A walk before breakfast, to help her put things in perspective.

Outside, the streets smelled fresh from the overnight rain. She walked aimlessly up the High Street, past quaint half-timbered Elizabethan shopfronts, interspersed with modern plate glass windows displaying winter coats and boots. Delivery vans were starting to arrive, bleary-eyed staff opening up shops as the sky lightened to a pale grey. Helen turned down a narrow alleyway lined with gift shops and cafes. At the end was the imposing gateway to the cathedral close, three storeys of stone carved with heraldic shields and angels.

The massive wooden gates were shut. Helen was disappointed; she'd hoped to be able to stroll around the cathedral grounds, even if the building itself was closed. Instead, she wandered around the old Butter Market, with the big stone war memorial in the centre.

A sound caught her ear and she turned back to the cathedral gatehouse. A small wooden door to the side of it swung open. Perhaps she would have a chance to see inside, after all.

'Hello. Are you opening up?' she asked.

A tall man in black church robes with a thin but friendly face turned to smile. 'Not to visitors, I'm afraid. Visits start at ten. But we will be holding Matins at half past seven. You're very welcome to join us for the service.'

Helen considered. She'd not been a churchgoer since childhood and had no religious faith. But she was curious to see the cathedral at this early hour, and she respected the faith of others. It would do no harm to sit quietly and listen.

'Thank you. I'd like that,' she said.

She stepped through the gate. The cathedral was huge, a soaring monument to centuries of craftsmanship. The stone shone pale gold in the floodlights, the towers sending their graceful pinnacles high into the lightening sky.

'You forget how impressive it is close up,' she said. 'I've not been here for a while.' She followed the man across the close.

'Are you visiting Canterbury?' he asked.

'I came to see a play at the Marlowe Theatre last night. I go back to London today.'

He raised his eyebrows. 'The play about Saint Thomas Becket? I'm going next week. Is it good?'

Helen grinned. 'It's amazing. But it doesn't paint Becket in a very flattering light. I hope you're not disappointed.'

He laughed. 'There are bigger things to worry about than whether someone is rude about a long-dead saint in a play. Even our saint.'

He opened a door in the cathedral porch. 'I'm Derek Bryce, the librarian canon. I'm acting vice dean this week. The resident canons take it in turns to do the early morning services.'

'Does that mean you get to live here?' asked Helen, noticing the handsome buildings that lined the cathedral close. 'Lucky you.'

'I know,' he said, his voice mischievous. 'It's a tough job. Better yet, I get to work in the library. It's a fascinating place.'

Helen tipped her head back to take in the lofty height of the nave, slim pillars raising the vaulted ceiling skywards, as she followed the canon through the cathedral.

'This is wonderful.' She found herself whispering as she listened to the echo of their footsteps. She wondered if he got used to it, being alone in the huge, empty space.

'Matins takes place in the crypt, the Jesus Chapel. We're a little early, but come down with me and I'll get set up,' he said.

Helen tried to take in the glory of the huge building as she hurried after him. Canon Bryce walked briskly along the side aisle and down a set of stone stairs.

'This is the oldest part of the cathedral,' he said. 'The crypt is the least-changed part of the building. Saint Thomas himself would recognise the western crypt.'

In the low light, Helen had trouble making out much detail. The vaulted roof, rich with carving, rested on a profusion of pillars like a stone forest supporting a leafy canopy. It was cold, with a dusty smell that made her think uncomfortably of the contents of the tombs they passed.

'Just through here…' The man stopped abruptly, and Helen almost walked into him. Her foot skidded on something wet. She lost her balance, went down awkwardly on one knee and reached out her hand to save herself. It was sticky. A pool of something wet and sticky on the stone floor. Helen raised her fingers to her nose, recoiled at the metallic taint.

The canon cried out and turned away, hands pressed to his face.

A figure in a grey suit was stretched out on the stone flags, head resting in a black lake of blood.

CHAPTER EIGHT

The man lay on his back, his face towards the altar, arms spread wide like a crucifixion. His throat gaped where it had been sliced across, ragged edges of skin exposing shockingly raw flesh. The cut was so deep that his head was barely attached to his body.

Helen stared, her mind stalling as she tried to make sense of the scene. It was not the first time she had seen a dead body. But she had never seen such savage violence before. She stepped back, put out a hand to steady herself against a marble pillar.

Right above the carnage, the early morning light caught the translucent shape of a human figure, as if the man's soul was hovering above him. She gasped, then realised it was a sculpture, suspended from the vaulted ceiling.

'Dear God.' Canon Bryce dropped to his knees beside the man and picked up his wrist. He looked up at Helen, his eyes wide with bewilderment. 'What's happened? I don't understand.'

'Is he dead?' The stupid words were out before Helen could bite them back. Of course he was dead.

'I think so.' The canon laid the man's arm back down. 'Yes.' He seemed stunned, unsure what to do next.

Helen moved to his side, saw the face. 'Oh! Oh, no.'

'What?'

'It's Mr Danbury. He lives at Harbledown.'

Canon Bryce nodded. 'Yes, I know. William.' He passed his hand over his face. 'He volunteers at the cathedral. I saw him… just the other day. Tuesday. I talked to him. I was going to call him today.'

He rubbed his eyes, as if trying to erase the sight before him. Then he bowed his head and muttered a few words of prayer. He breathed a quick 'Amen' and got slowly to his feet.

'Right. I suppose I should get the constables. Would you – would you mind staying with him, Helen? I don't think we should leave him. I'll be as quick as I can.'

Helen swallowed down the panic rising in her chest. Who had done this? Where were they now? She really didn't want to be left alone.

'All right.' She hoped he wouldn't be long. 'Is there anything I can do?'

The man sighed. 'Pray for him,' he said.

Helen stood with her back to the shiny marble pillar, needing something solid behind her. The ring of Canon Bryce's hurrying footsteps died away, and a profound silence descended. She strained her ears and scanned the shadows, alert for any flicker of movement. They could still be here, she wanted to shout after the canon. The people who did this. Don't leave me with them.

The copper taint of blood hung in the cold air. She breathed in shallow gulps, not wanting the corruption of it in her lungs. Her left hand was wet and she held it awkwardly away from her, trying not to get blood on her clothes.

She did not pray. Years ago, she had abandoned her faith in

43

anything out there capable of hearing a prayer. There were no gods, no demons. But something profoundly evil was present in this place that humanity had made sacred.

She'd met William Danbury only once, at Harbledown, on the fateful day when she arrived at the church. He had been brisk, friendly but distant. He, like his neighbour Alice, had been a guardian of the final burial place of Thomas Becket, and was now master of Eastbridge. Helen thought of Alice, imagined her distress at this terrible news.

She didn't want to look at his ravaged body. She fixed her gaze on the strange sculpture above him, suspended by wires like a mummified bundle above the ground. She knew the style: the sculptor Antony Gormley. The sculpture was made up of hundreds of nails, fixed together to indicate the mass of the human form. What was it doing here?

She glanced around the crypt again, but the shadows were still, unmoving. Above her head, the windows had started to shine. William Danbury's face caught the light, his skin pale grey like putty. Light gleamed off the dark blood around him. Helen noticed one knee of her jeans was stained where she'd lost her balance and fallen.

She shuddered. Trying to distract herself, she bent to read the small notice explaining the eerie artwork. The nails had been salvaged from the cathedral itself during restoration work. And its position was very deliberate.

The sculpture hung above the spot where Saint Thomas Becket was first laid to rest, immediately after his murder. The monks had placed his tomb here in the crypt, before the ornate shrine was built in the body of the cathedral two centuries later.

And now, William's body, horribly mutilated, lay where

Becket's corpse once lay.

With relief, Helen heard loud voices and heavy footsteps from the stairwell. Canon Bryce, accompanied by two middle-aged police officers.

'Thank you for staying, Helen,' said the canon. 'Are you all right? The cathedral constables will secure the crypt until Kent Police arrive. Let's go upstairs. It's been a shock.'

Helen followed him up the stairs and out of the cathedral into watery sunshine. It seemed an age since they had entered the vast building.

'The police want to talk to us both,' said the canon. 'We can wait in my house. I'll make coffee. I'm sure we could both do with some.'

'Thank you.' Helen shivered, as if the penetrating cold of the crypt had only now entered her bones.

'The cathedral constables are a separate force,' Canon Bryce explained. 'They patrol the cathedral close. Anything as serious as this and we call in the Kent force.'

Helen nodded. 'A town within a town,' she said, taking in the lawns and redbrick houses ringing the cathedral. The peaceful scene seemed unreal, an idyllic stage backdrop startlingly at odds with the horrors in the crypt. 'Your own police force. The gates locked all night.' That must cut down the suspects, she thought. Depending on who had the keys.

'True.' Canon Bryce led the way across the close. A gang of small boys was being shepherded into minibuses, as if nothing out of the ordinary had happened. Run, Helen wanted to tell them. Get out of here, it's not safe.

'We even have our own schools, as you can see. This lot sing in the choir. That's Choir House, by the ruins of the old cloister.' He pointed to a flint-faced building opposite a row of tumbledown arches.

Helen heard a whoop of sirens and turned to see a police van rounding the corner. A cathedral constable waved it towards the main cathedral door.

A small boy detached himself from the contingent being loaded into the buses and ran over to them. 'What's happening?' He saw Helen and stopped. 'Hello again.'

It was the chorister from last night's performance.

'Hello,' she said, trying to remember his name. 'You were brilliant last night.'

'Of course,' said the canon. 'It was your big night, wasn't it, Joshua? Did it go well?'

'Yeah. What's going on? Why are the police here?'

Canon Bryce's smile became a little forced. 'Nothing to worry about. Go on, you'll miss the bus.' His voice had an overly hearty tone.

The boy gazed over at the police running into the cathedral. 'People always say that when there is something to worry about,' he grumbled.

Helen saw him switch his gaze to her left hand. A question formed in his face. She clenched her fist, longing to wash off the blood, and looked away.

'I'll find out in the end.' He joined the others on the bus.

They watched it drive away.

'Why do you think Mr Danbury's body was placed where Thomas Becket's tomb used to be?' asked Helen. 'Don't you think that's strange?'

The man let out a long sigh. 'I have absolutely no idea.'

Helen looked at him sharply. His voice had the same slightly false tone he'd used to try to reassure Josh. Like Josh, she wasn't sure that she believed him. She followed him into the elegant

Georgian house, wondering.

CHAPTER NINE

'Over here, Helen.'

Henry waved from the breakfast bar in the hotel lobby. He was wearing a big green jersey and chomping his way through bacon, eggs, sausage and beans.

'Have you had breakfast yet? Come and join me. Nothing like a full English for settling a hangover. We had quite a party last night.'

Helen's stomach lurched. She'd not eaten since the previous night, and it was almost ten o'clock. The coffee she'd drunk while waiting for the police churned uneasily. Maybe some toast would be a good idea. She sat opposite Henry, trying not to look at the remains of the greasy meat on his plate.

'What's up? You look like you've seen a ghost.'

She sighed. 'Not far off.' She helped herself to tea. 'Could I have some toast?' she asked a hovering waitress. 'I don't really want a cooked breakfast.'

Between mouthfuls, she filled him in on the discovery of William Danbury's body.

'God, that's awful. And you knew this chap?'

'Well, I only met him once. But I liked him.'

'What do they think it was – heart attack?'

Helen swallowed her toast. 'No. The police think he was

killed deliberately.'

Given the state of his body, Helen couldn't imagine how it could be anything but murder. The police had asked her not to talk about the manner of his death, or how the body had looked when it was found. And telling Henry would be the quickest way to tell the entire theatre company.

'Shit! Really? What was it, some kind of Satanic ritual? Black magic and all that?' Henry's eyes were bright. He looked like an excited kid.

'No. I don't know. I don't think so.' She'd overheard one of the police officers make the same suggestion to his colleague over the radio. But grim as it was, she didn't think Satanism was at the root of the murder. It was something to do with Becket, she felt sure of that.

'Poor you. As if that business last night wasn't upsetting enough, without going around finding corpses in the crypt. Shall we get some croissants?'

Helen really wasn't in the mood for Henry. She finished her tea and reached for her bag.

'Not for me. I want to see a friend before I head back to London. I hope the rest of the run goes well,' she said.

Helen planned to walk up to Harbledown and see Alice Delamare in person, rather than calling by phone first. Alice would be distressed by the news of William's death. It would be better to go and see her than to try to give her condolences by phone. Maybe she should take flowers.

'Hello.' Gregory Hall arrived at their table, unshaven and rumple-headed, but still handsome.

'Hi.' Helen sat back down. He pulled up a chair. His expressive face was crumpled with worry.

'Something's up, Henry. I'm concerned.' He pulled out his

phone. 'Someone sent me this on Twitter. It's been taken down already, but my agent saw it and took a screenshot before he reported it. And I've just seen on TV that someone has been found dead in the cathedral.'

He passed the phone to Henry.

'Shit. That's a bit... Helen, what time did it happen? The discovery of the body this morning?'

The director showed her the phone. On the screen, an image of a police van driving in at the cathedral gate. Above it, a message: '@The_Greg_Hall you are next. Every performance of that filthy play = one dead body. #defendchristianity'

Oh, God. Did this mean the death of William Danbury was linked to Christopher Marlowe's play?

Helen looked at the timestamp on the message: 07.34am. About ten minutes after she and Canon Bryce found William's body. The photograph must have been taken around the time she and the canon emerged from the cathedral, just as the police arrived. So whoever took that photograph had been outside the cathedral gate, waiting for the corpse to be discovered.

'You should take this to the police,' she said.

She thought back to her own arrival at the cathedral. She'd mooched around the Butter Market, read the names on the war memorial. She didn't remember seeing anyone else. The thought gave her the creeps. Had they been hidden in a doorway, somewhere along the narrow alleyway she had walked down minutes earlier?

'Why? What do you know?' Greg's emerald eyes fixed on Helen.

'This was taken just after we discovered the body,' she said. 'Whoever took it knew the police would be on their way.'

'You discovered it?' His eyebrows shot up.

'I went to the early service at the cathedral. I was the first one there, with the priest leading the service. And we found the poor man in the crypt,' she said.

'Ach, that's awful. What a shock for you.' His voice was soft. Helen's eyes were suddenly full of tears. She looked away and reached for a tissue.

'Sorry. It was a bit upsetting. But this could be important. I mean… if his death is somehow connected to the play? To the protestors?'

He put his warm palm over her hand. 'When are you going to tell me more about this play, then? I knew there was something.' His smile was teasing.

She pulled her hand away, flushing hot from her toes up. 'Nothing to tell,' she said.

Henry was on his feet. 'Helen's right, Greg. This is serious. I'm not having threats against my production, or my actors. We'll call the police from my room.'

He hugged Helen. 'You look after yourself, my darling. I'll give you a call later and tell you what's happening.'

'Don't go home yet,' Greg told her. 'Can we have lunch?'

Helen hesitated, her willpower swiftly eroding. 'I have to go and see a friend. I don't know what time I'll be back.'

'Does Henry have your number? I'll call you,' he said.

The two men departed. Helen still felt the warmth of Greg's hand. Her heart was thumping. But there was no time for daydreaming. She had things to do. If she walked up to Harbledown now, she could be back before lunchtime and still make it home to Deptford by the middle of the afternoon.

Maybe.

She longed suddenly for the seclusion of her little flat, up

51

above the trees with a view over the rooftops. Insulated with books, the shelves overflowing with them. Her refuge against the world. She'd be back soon. But she owed it to Alice to see her first.

CHAPTER TEN

Helen walked up the hill to Harbledown village, past pleasant villas and cottages. It was only a couple of miles from Canterbury city centre, but felt rural. The trees and hedgerows smelled fresh and damp in the sunshine. The day was warming up and she had started to feel too hot in her sweater.

She turned off the road and walked up the steps to the gateway to St Nicholas's Church. She paused a moment, getting her breath back and surveying the tranquil grounds. The alms houses – once a medieval leper hospital – were to the side of the church, opening onto a smooth green lawn.

Helen remembered her first visit, as she'd followed her quest to its conclusion. Mr Danbury had been reading a newspaper, sitting in a folding chair outside his house. Alice Delamere had been gardening, potting up new plants. She'd taken the big key from her basket and let Helen into the church.

Once again, she thought, she was arriving to bring trouble to this peaceful spot. She didn't know whether Alice would have heard of her neighbour's death already, or whether she would be breaking the news herself. Either way, Helen feared her friend would be distraught.

The dark wooden doors to the alms houses were all shut.

Helen went to the second one along, with big pots of herbs ranged in front of it, and rang the bell. She could see Alice's kitchen through the leaded window, tidy and cheerful with a bunch of chrysanthemums in a blue jug on the table.

No answer. Helen rang again and waited. She wasn't sure how good Alice's hearing was. She peered through the window. No sign of used coffee cups. No breakfast dishes drying in the rack next to the sink.

She bent to call through the letterbox. It was partially wedged open, a newspaper not quite pushed through.

Helen pulled out her phone. Half past eleven. Alice didn't strike her as someone who would lie late in bed. She scrolled through to Alice's number. She could hear the phone ringing from inside the house. It rang five times, then the answerphone kicked in; Alice's bright voice politely inviting her to leave a message.

'It's Helen Oddfellow. I'm outside your house. Are you in? Can you get to the door?'

Helen began to feel worried. Had Alice fallen and hurt herself? Was she lying inside the house ill, or injured, unable to get up?

The door beyond Mr Danbury's house opened and an elderly woman wearing a floral patterned housecoat looked out.

'Have you come about William?' she asked. 'Is it true?'

Helen hesitated. 'I'm looking for Alice. Have you seen her?'

'I don't know. But what about William? The police have been round. Someone said he's dead.'

Helen sighed. 'I'm afraid he is. But I'm worried about Alice. She's not answering her door.'

The woman clasped her hands. 'That's awful. Was it his heart?'

54

Helen wasn't going to go into details. 'I don't know. I'm very sorry. You were friends?'

She nodded, vigorously. 'Oh, yes. He kept this place on its toes. Up to scratch. He didn't let anyone get away with any nonsense.'

Remembering William's upright posture and briskness, Helen could imagine it. 'I'm so sorry,' she repeated. 'But I am a bit worried about Alice. Have you seen her today?'

The woman put her head on one side, considered. 'Yes. No, wait. I think it was yesterday. She was getting the bus, and she had to come back for her umbrella because of the rain. Isn't she back yet?'

Helen realised she'd not seen Alice at all at the theatre. She'd assumed she left early, but had she even arrived?

'Thanks. Look, is there a warden I can call? I think we should check she's not had a fall or something.'

The warden was there in fifteen minutes, a man in his twenties wearing sweatpants and trainers.

'You all right, Eva?' he asked the woman, who'd come out of her door again to watch. 'I'll come by and say hello later, yeah?' The woman smiled and retreated indoors.

'What a day,' he said. 'I've been with the police, sorting out next of kin stuff for one of the residents who's passed on. I'm Terry, by the way. Thanks for calling. Let's have a check inside.'

He knocked, unlocked the door and opened it. 'Hello?' he called. 'Alice, I'm just going to check your bedroom.'

It took seconds to establish that the four-room dwelling was empty, the bed neatly made.

'That's weird,' he said. 'They usually let me know if they're going to be away for the night.'

'That lady – Eva?' said Helen. 'She said Alice left for

Canterbury yesterday in the afternoon. She was going to the theatre. I was there, and I looked for her afterwards, but I thought she must have left before the end.'

'Huh.' Terry leaned against the wall. 'That's weird, too. William – that's the resident who died – was going to the theatre yesterday. They hung out together a lot, William and Alice. I wonder if they were planning to go together?'

Helen flashed back to the previous night. She'd been on stage, had given her speech. She'd looked around the audience, seen two empty seats in the middle of the stalls. Alice, and maybe William. William was dead. The question was, where was Alice?

'I think we'd better call the police,' she said. 'I have a bad feeling about this. If Alice and William were together... and William...' She broke off. She didn't know how much the man had been told about William's death.

'Yeah,' he said. 'They told me. Suspected murder, in the cathedral. Come on, I'll drive you down to the police station.'

CHAPTER ELEVEN

The desk sergeant at Canterbury police station picked up the phone as soon as Helen said she had information connected to William Danbury's murder. 'Take a seat. I'll see who's around. They'll have appointed an investigating officer by now.'

Helen paced the waiting area, too wired to sit on the metal bench. Minutes later, a familiar voice summoned her from a side door.

'Helen Oddfellow. What have you got yourself involved in this time?'

It was a woman in her forties, with short greying hair, a neat navy trouser suit and black lace-up shoes. Her stern look was betrayed by a half-smile of welcome.

'Sarah! What are you doing here?' She'd last seen Detective Chief Inspector Sarah Greenley more than a year ago, when the woman had still been working out of Deptford police station.

'I got myself a new job. I was hoping for a quiet life in a genteel cathedral city.' The policewoman raised her eyebrows. 'That's going well. Come through. Fill me in. Front desk say you've got a missing person to add to our murder inquiry.'

They sat in Sarah Greenley's cubbyhole of an office, utilitarian with bare walls and grey furniture. It was a huge relief to

Helen to know the investigation was in capable hands. Quickly, Helen filled her in on the details.

'Alice Delamare is William's next-door neighbour. She left her home yesterday afternoon to go to the performance at the Marlowe Theatre. I was there and I don't think she arrived. She's not been home since. And the warden says William had planned to go to the theatre, too, so we thought they might have gone together. And, of course, you know what's happened to William, so I thought…'

'Right. We'll check with the theatre box office about tickets.' Sarah looked up from her notes, a frown bisecting her brow. 'Do you know how she was travelling? Did she have a car?'

'No. Her neighbour said she was going to get the bus. Sometime in the afternoon.'

'Fine. We'll check that out.' Sarah pushed back her chair and observed Helen with level brown eyes.

'Now. Tell me the rest. Why do you think this happened? What was it you were telling the officers this morning about William Danbury and Eastbridge Hospital? Don't tell me this is linked to that business with Gary Paxton.'

Helen trusted the policewoman, but didn't want to give away secrets that were not hers to give.

'William Danbury and Alice Delamare were there when Francis Nash died,' she said. 'Nash thought they knew something. A secret. Alice's late husband was master of Eastbridge, and William is the current master. Was, I mean. So, anything that Eastbridge Hospital knows, they know.'

Sarah nodded. 'All right. And this secret is?'

Helen blushed and lied. 'I don't know exactly. But it's about Thomas Becket. And William's body – we found it where Becket's tomb once stood.'

Sarah held her eyes a moment longer. Helen had the feeling her secrets were being penetrated by willpower alone.

'And there was the protest at the theatre,' she added, reluctantly. 'The play about Thomas Becket. I wondered if that could be linked.'

'You should tell me everything,' the woman said. 'I'll find out anyway. Saves time. Could save lives. You know that.'

They sat in uncomfortable silence for a moment. Sarah sighed.

'Let me put out the word about your missing person,' she said. 'Then you can tell me what happened at the theatre. I understand someone was brought in for questioning last night. He's been released, but we can pull him back in if need be.'

Sarah went through to the investigation room. Helen pictured Alice, bright blue eyes below her blunt silver fringe, setting out for the bus with her umbrella. The performance hadn't been due to start until seven-thirty. Eva said Alice had left in the afternoon, so where had she gone in the meantime? Shopping, perhaps. Eastbridge, maybe. Had she met William there? And then what had happened?

'Right.' Sarah was back. 'Apparently there's been a threat to one of the actors, too. Did you know about that?'

Helen remembered the message on Gregory Hall's phone. She nodded. 'It's all tied together, I think. The disruption of the play. William's murder. Alice's disappearance, and the death threat.'

'Go on, then,' said Sarah. 'Spill it.'

Helen leaned forward, her elbows on the desk between them. 'I think it's to do with the current burial place of Thomas Becket. There's no official record of what happened to his body after Henry VIII had the shrine destroyed. But Eastbridge Hospital knows about it. The Marlowe play hints at it. And it's what Father Nash was trying to find out when he died.

'The guy at the theatre last night called it a "filthy play". That's what Father Nash called it, because it trashes Becket's reputation. So my guess is, all of this has something to do with Nash's old organisation, Christianity in Crisis.'

The policewoman was taking notes. 'We looked into the group at the time. Francis Nash was the driving force. He was funded largely by Lady Joan Brooke. They're both dead. No-one else had access to the money. The rest of them seemed harmless enough. Mainly pensioners, plenty of dodgy attitudes, but nothing criminal.'

'Still, I bet the guy last night was involved with Christianity in Crisis,' said Helen. 'And the protestors outside the theatre.'

'Good point,' said Sarah. 'We'll check. If they're working together again, someone must have galvanised them. We need to find out who's in charge. But waving a placard is a long way from abduction and murder. The team is still searching the cathedral, so they'll look for any signs of Mrs Delamare, too. How long are you in Canterbury?'

'Damn.' Helen looked at her watch. 'I was supposed to check out of the hotel half an hour ago. I planned to go back to London today.'

'OK. Same address and phone number?'

'Yeah.' Helen didn't want to go back with Alice still missing. She felt somehow responsible. But the hotel was expensive and she'd only stayed there because the theatre was paying. Maybe she could find somewhere else for another night.

'Here. Take my mobile number. I might stay around for a bit,' she said.

Sarah pocketed the scrap of paper and handed over her card.

As Helen rose to go, she leaned back in her chair, frowning.

'Helen. Listen to me. Don't get involved. We'll do all we can to find Alice. All right? Go back to London. Stay out of trouble. I mean it.'

Helen smiled. 'I know you do.'

She left the police station, crossed the ring road and headed back into the city centre.

CHAPTER TWELVE

Helen swung her rucksack onto her back, left the hotel and walked down the High Street. She wasn't sure where she was going. Police stood at the gates of the cathedral, which had been closed to visitors. She wished she could go in and help them search. Much as she trusted Sarah Greenley, she'd seen the size of the cathedral and the scale of the task. More than anything, she wanted to do something that might help to find Alice.

She checked her phone. One missed call, number withheld. She listened to the answerphone message.

'Hi, it's Greg. If you're back in time, meet me for lunch at the café opposite the theatre, one o'clock.'

It was almost two. Damn, thought Helen, would he think she'd been ignoring him? Running her hands through her hair, she quickly turned her steps towards the theatre. She checked the café, but it was disappointingly empty.

She paused outside the theatre. Would the box office tell her if Alice had picked up her ticket? She might as well give it a try.

'I want to check whether my friend made it to the performance last night,' she told the girl at the desk. 'I was meant to meet her afterwards and couldn't find her.'

The girl looked through the previous evening's reserved tickets. 'Delamare. Sorry, nothing under that name,' she said.

Helen thought again. 'Could you try another name? She was going with a friend. William Danbury.'

The girl returned to the card index. 'Danbury. Yes, here you are. Two tickets for last night's performance. Not collected.'

Helen's heart sank. A scrap of hope that it might have been a mistake, that Alice may have had other arrangements, disappeared.

'OK. Thanks for looking.'

As she crossed the foyer, she passed two uniformed police officers on their way in, presumably on the same mission. Hastily, she exited the building.

She walked around the glass and steel box that housed the theatre, pausing by the old brick bridge over the river. She leaned on the parapet and looked down to the emerald strands of weed streaming in the water, the colour of Gregory Hall's eyes.

The River Stour was shallow and gin-clear, very different from the cocoa-coloured Thames that she knew so well. It looked newer, younger. Yet this river, too, had flowed through its city for thousands of years. She wanted to run her fingers through its clear stream, roll up her jeans and wade in. To wash off the taint of evil that had clung to her since the discovery in the crypt.

'Hello, Helen.' She jumped. A man had appeared next to her.

He was in late middle age, skinny with a straggly beard and greasy hair that reached his collar. His zip-up fleece looked grubby and had a musty smell. Helen couldn't place him. Was he with the theatre? One of the cast, perhaps, or a stagehand.

'Are you all right? After last night, I mean,' he asked.

'Yes, thank you.' She didn't want to get into a conversation about the attack with a stranger.

'That's good. It wasn't meant to hurt you. It was only fake, you know. Fake blood for a fake play.'

Shit. She turned to look at him properly. 'You?'

He cast his eyes down shyly, as if too modest to admit to the attack. 'I'm afraid so.'

Helen took a step back. 'But what on earth... why did you do it? The play's not a forgery. It's genuinely by Christopher Marlowe. You might not like it, but that's no reason to chuck stuff at me.'

He smiled, showing protruding yellowed teeth. It was not an attractive sight.

'You should respect the memory of Saint Thomas,' he said. 'I was doing the work of the Lord. Do not obstruct the work of the Lord.'

Helen shuddered. She'd heard those words before. 'Get away from me,' she said, walking briskly back towards the theatre. 'Or I'll call the police.'

'We'll win in the end,' he called.

She stopped.

'Who is "we"?' she asked, turning to face him. 'Who's in charge of your little gang?' Whoever it was might know about the murder of William Danbury. And even more importantly, about what had happened to Alice.

He walked over to join her. 'Let's sit here for a chat,' he said, indicating a bench on the riverside path.

Helen didn't want to be anywhere near the man. He gave her the absolute creeps. But she thought about the two uncollected tickets and the chrysanthemums on Alice's kitchen table. She wanted to know what this man knew. She sat right at the end of the bench, ready to run.

'Go on, then,' she said. 'Who told you to stage that protest?'

'No-one tells me to do anything,' he said, tetchily. 'The blood was my idea. I thought it would be dramatic.'

'All right. Very dramatic. But what about the rest of the protestors? Who organised them? Was it you?'

He scuffed his feet in the gravel. She got the feeling he'd like to have claimed to be the organiser.

'We each have a role. Father Nash might be dead. But we're not.'

So, they were from Francis Nash's crackpot group of followers.

'Christianity in Crisis? You're still going, then. Who's the leader now?'

He shook his head. 'We're not stupid. We know what happened to Father Nash in the church. They said it was an accident. We know who we hold responsible, Helen Oddfellow. We're not going to risk losing another leader.'

'It was an accident.' Helen didn't want to think about Francis Nash's death.

'So you say. So they said. It's not their first cover-up, is it?' said the man.

'Who do you think is covering it up?' asked Helen. She knew the answer already.

'Eastbridge,' he said, spitting the word out like a curse. 'Eastbridge, of course.'

'You should talk to the master, then,' she said. 'Mr Danbury. Take it up with him.'

He looked at her sideways, his smile shifty. 'Haven't you heard?' he asked. 'The master is dead.'

William's name had not been released publicly, as far as

Helen understood. But enough people already knew about it – his neighbours, people at the cathedral – that the news could conceivably have leaked out. What else did this man know? she wondered.

'Tell me more.'

'I've told you enough.' He got to his feet. 'Watch yourself, Helen Oddfellow. That play is ungodly. It must never be performed again.'

He walked away, down the river path. Helen watched him go. Every performance equals one dead body, Gregory Hall had been told. Had she just been given the same warning? She wondered if she should call Sarah Greenley, tell the policewoman about the encounter. Sarah had said the police might bring the protestor back for further questioning. Perhaps she should know that he'd already known about William Danbury's death.

Helen crossed to the other side of the bridge, watching the water making its way down past the ancient buildings. The next bridge along, she realised, was Eastbridge. The river flowed right under Eastbridge Hospital, next to the dank undercroft where Canterbury's pilgrims had once rested their bones after their long journey to the city. As she watched, a flat-bottomed punt slid by, a huddle of tourists shrieking with excitement as the boat headed under the bridge.

Helen took her phone from her pocket to call Sarah. One new message, with a photograph attached. Frowning, she opened it.

It was a blurry photograph of her, taken from the back. She was standing next to the Butter Market cross, the image grainy in the early morning light. Two words in the message, which came from a withheld number.

'You're next.'

The day suddenly felt colder. Helen stared at the image. Someone had been there, watching her.

'Hey!' a familiar voice called from the theatre steps. Gregory Hall strode across the plaza in jeans and a hoodie, a big smile on his face. 'You stood me up.'

She tried to laugh. 'Sorry. Stuff got in the way. I only just got your message.'

He looked harder at her. 'What's up? You don't look very happy about it.'

Helen turned the phone towards him. 'That wasn't the only message.' She showed him the image.

'Shit. You got one too.'

Helen nodded, tried to keep calm. 'And the friend I went to see – I couldn't find her. I think something might have happened to her. I'm… I'm a bit scared.'

'Hey, now.' His eyes were kind. 'Course you are. Tell me what's been happening.'

Helen fought the urge to lean against him. Stop being ridiculous, she told herself.

'OK. But let's go to the Butter Market. I want to see where this was taken from,' she said.

CHAPTER THIRTEEN

Alice sat on the wooden floor, her bones aching. Pale sun filtered through the narrow windows, illuminating the whitewashed walls and the white-draped altar. It was quiet; almost silent. She could just hear the trickle of the stream running below the building.

She'd watched the shadows shift across the uneven oak floorboards since first light. It was past noon now, maybe a long time past. It was hard to keep track.

An icon of the Virgin Mary, next to a crucifix, looked down at her with indifference. She'd failed. She had not been able to raise the alarm, or call the constables. The horrible giant had taken William and she had not seen him since. The mysterious woman had barely spoken after they left. She gagged Alice; told her she would give her time to think about what she wanted to say. Then, later, the man had returned and she'd been trussed like a Sunday roast, shoved into a trolley, bumped and jolted around. He'd carried her up the stairs to the chapel and dumped her here without a word.

He had not answered her pleas to tell her what he had done with William. It had been pitch dark and Alice had been close to despair. He untied her bonds, gave her a cheese sandwich and a bottle of water, then left. She'd been alone ever since.

She heard footsteps on the path outside and slowly pulled herself to her feet, joints sore from the hard floor. She went to the window, but could see no-one. Only the meadow, a sea of seed heads and grasses, browned by autumn and bowed by the rain.

She heard a door creak open downstairs, footsteps on the stairway. She held her breath, pressed herself back against the wall. But the door to the upstairs chapel remained shut.

'Good afternoon, Alice. I thought it was time to try again,' said the woman from outside the door. She sounded tired, her accent coming through the careful enunciation. The accent was north Kent, the distinctive drawl that sounded to Alice as if the speaker was constantly complaining. It took her back to Chatham, the Victorian parish church where she and Mark had spent almost twenty years. Was that it? Did she know this woman from St Augustine's?

'Where's William?' she asked.

'Forget about William,' the woman said.

'What have you done with him? He needs to go to hospital,' she said.

'He's been taken care of.' The woman's voice took on a suppressed excitement, almost as if she was trying not to laugh. Alice found that more disturbing than if she'd shouted in anger. 'It's just the two of us,' said the voice. 'Things go better when the women are in charge, don't they? Let's keep this between ourselves.'

Alice had a sudden dizzying waft of déjà vu. The sharp pine smell of disinfectant on a varnished floor. Harsh fluorescent lighting. Dampness, umbrellas dripping in the corner and a pile of wet coats. The hall of St Augustine's church.

As the vicar's wife, Alice had been expected to serve alongside her husband, to be the archetypal cake-baking flower-arranging Sunday-school-teaching paragon of virtue. She'd fallen way short of that expectation, spending long hours reading and studying in the 1960s pebble-dashed bungalow that served as the vicarage. She'd completed her master's degree in the influence of Islam on medieval Christian thought. She'd stubbornly resisted the pressure to teach Sunday school, finding the upbringing of their own two boys demanding enough without taking on the Christian education of the whole parish. But she had agreed to chair the Mothers' Union, hoping it would introduce her to some helpful babysitters.

The light flickered on the floor, diffused by the trees ringing the meadow. Alice remembered the day she'd first met Jean Forbes. It must have been the mid-1980s, more than thirty years ago. The young woman had arrived early for the meeting, tall and rather beautiful in skin-tight jeans and high-heeled boots, dragging along a pair of reluctant school children.

'Sit there and shut up,' she'd told them, pointing to a corner of the hall. They'd dragged a couple of metal chairs from the stacks around the room, sagging canvas seats frayed at the edges.

The young woman had turned to Alice, an unconvincing smile on her harried face. 'They won't be any trouble. My husband isn't home yet. I don't want them playing out with the kids from the estate.' She'd aspirated hard on her aitches, as if she'd only just learned to pronounce them.

The children hadn't been any trouble. Jean, on the other hand, had brought scandal and division to the parish. Alice had tried to befriend her at first, feeling sorry for the young woman who seemed to have little support from her husband, struggling with a sulky girl and a younger boy who rarely spoke.

70

But Jean Forbes had proven a hard woman to like.

Was it really her? And if so… Alice's mind flicked back to the previous day, Derek Bryce stopping her in the cloister. He'd wanted to ask her about something, and she'd put him off. Damn.

'Jean,' she said. 'From Chatham. Isn't it?'

There was a pause. Then: 'Rochester, actually. You've recovered your memory, then.' The voice regained a little of its former harshness, as if the woman, too, had stepped back in time. Alice heard the lock turn and the door opened.

The woman didn't look old. But she didn't look young, either. She must be in her sixties, Alice supposed. Jean was what people called 'well preserved', as if she'd been frozen or pickled. Her hair was shorter, a more sophisticated cut, but still the same shade of ash blonde. Her skin was smooth, except for a few wrinkles around the lips and eyes. She wore subtle make-up, the sort only other women noticed.

'I do remember you, Jean.' Alice tried to keep her voice gentle. 'I always wondered what had happened to you. I'm sorry we parted on unfriendly terms.'

'Well, now you know. And you can tell me what else you know, about Saint Thomas and his burial place. If you don't want to wind up like your friend.'

A stone formed in Alice's chest. She swallowed, forced the words out through her dry mouth.

'What have you done to William? Where is he?'

'I did warn him.' Jean sounded defensive. 'They've found him now. In the cathedral. I heard it on the news.'

The stone swelled, hard and painful, squeezing the breath from her. William. That kind, decent, brave man. Alice pressed the palms of her hands to her eyes. She would weep for him, but not in the presence of this woman. Alice knew too well the work of mourning, its depths and distance. She took her last memory of him, the touch of her lips on his skin, and folded it small.

'You killed him.' The strength of her voice, the anger, surprised her. She slapped her hand against the wall. 'You bloody killed him.'

'I didn't,' said Jean, the emphasis on the word 'I'. She sounded hurt. 'But I warned him, didn't I? About what would happen if he didn't do what I said. He should have listened to me. Like you should, Alice. People should just learn to listen to me.'

Alice crossed to the window. She didn't want to hear this woman's whining. She remembered it all too well: the false chumminess that descended quickly into grievance, the desire to be seen as important. She remembered the constant rows, the ridiculous fights over the flower arranging rota, Jean's hostility to other women. The awful threats to poor, deluded Derek, back when he was Mark's curate in Chatham.

But she never could have imagined the unpleasant young woman she'd met thirty years ago would have become a killer.

The scene outside was peaceful, a gentle sun warming the meadow grasses. Too peaceful; Alice knew the gardens were locked during the autumn and winter. They were opened once a week for a church service in the chapel, on a Wednesday. Today was Friday. Would anyone come in that time? A gardener, perhaps, to mow the long grass?

Part of Alice wanted to stay in this chapel forever, to weep for her friend. If she, too, was to die, then so be it. She was too tired, too old to fight.

But a hot core of anger was starting to glow, a desire to see this woman punished. She had to survive. She had to escape, to bring down justice on Jean's head.

Keep the faith, William had told her. Well, their faiths were perhaps different. In truth, Alice had little interest in protecting a pile of old bones. She did not believe in the sanctity of relics. Let other people turn over the bones of the dead. It was the living that concerned her now.

'If I were to tell you about Becket,' she said, 'you would have no reason not to kill me, too. So why should I help you? If I keep quiet, they'll find me. Now that they've found William.'

'They don't know about you,' the woman said. 'They don't even know you're missing, do they?'

Alice supposed not.

Mark was dead. Their sons lived abroad, busy and fulfilling lives. They spoke by phone, maybe once a fortnight. William was the person who checked in on her every day, made sure she was all right. She rested her aching head in her hands. Somehow, without her even realising it, William had become the most important presence in her life. And he was dead. She was on her own.

'Why do you care, Jean? What's Becket to you?' she asked. The woman hadn't shown any interest in history, or even Christianity, when they had known each other.

'Saint Thomas Becket,' Jean said, 'defended the church. And the church needs defending again, against the atheists and the Muslims and the liberals who think none of this matters.'

'You sound like Francis Nash,' said Alice. Had Jean been part of his potty group of followers? It might have appealed to her, she supposed. A group nominally dedicated to the defence of Christianity, but one which sought to exclude people, set up borders and barriers. For a woman with little power, little status, it could have been attractive.

'Father Nash was a martyr,' said Jean. 'You can kill one man, but you can't kill an idea. I will see to it that his work carries on. You should work with us. While you still can.'

Alice noted the threat in her words. She realised she should never have let Jean know she had recognised her voice. While Jean had thought herself anonymous, there had been a thread of hope that she might release her. But now Alice knew that Jean Forbes was responsible for William's death.

She's going to kill me, too, she realised, with absolute certainty. Unless I can escape, she's going to kill me.

CHAPTER FOURTEEN

H elen and Greg walked around the Butter Market, trying to work out where the photograph had been taken from. Helen had been standing to one side of the cross, her back to the camera, shops and cafes blurred but visible in the background.

'It looks to me like it was taken from the cathedral gate,' said Greg. 'Was it open when you arrived?'

Helen shook her head and frowned. She looked up at the dramatic carved stone gatehouse. Could someone have been up there, in the gatehouse itself? Surely not; it must have been taken from one of the adjacent doorways, perhaps one of the shops that stood on either side.

She crossed the square and stood in the doorway of the souvenir shop to the left of the gatehouse, lining up the view with the photo on her phone. It could have been, she supposed. But she might have turned and seen the photographer at any time. And she was pretty sure there had been no-one standing in the square when she arrived.

The uniformed policeman standing outside the cathedral gatehouse was watching her with suspicion. She walked over to him and smiled.

'The cathedral's still closed, is it?'

'That's right, madam.'

Madam. I must have aged, thought Helen. I'm sure police officers used to call me miss.

'Someone sent me this photo of myself,' she told him. 'I was trying to work out where it was taken from.'

He glanced at the screen. 'That's here, isn't it?'

'Exactly. This morning, about seven.' She waited for him to notice the implication.

'May I have a closer look?' He took the phone, glancing around the square. 'Who sent this to you?'

She shrugged. 'Number withheld. It's a bit odd, isn't it?'

'Why do you say that?'

'Because ten minutes later, I walked through this door for the Matins service and found the body of William Danbury in the crypt. And now it looks like someone was watching me, before I even went inside.'

'Hold on a sec. What's your name?' He started talking into his walkie-talkie radio.

Greg was looking at his watch. 'Sorry, Helen. I need to get back to the hotel. I've got a call with my agent, and then I need to get some sleep before the show.' He took her hand. 'Are you all right, now?'

The side door in the gatehouse opened.

'Come through, Helen,' said Sarah Greenley. Her voice was weary. 'I thought I'd told you to go home.' She looked with surprise at Greg, still holding Helen's hand. 'Are you coming, too, sir?'

'Not now.' He hesitated, then kissed Helen on the cheek. 'Look after yourself. I'll call you.'

Helen felt herself blushing from her boots upwards. She followed Sarah Greenley through the door.

'Sorry. I was on my way to the station. But a man came up and started talking to me, outside the theatre.'

'That man? Isn't he an actor?'

'Not him, no. It was the man who threw the blood at me last night. And he said he and the other protestors are part of the Christianity in Crisis group. Also, he already knew that William Danbury was dead.'

Sarah beckoned her away from the gate and they walked through the precincts where puddles lay on the grey flagstones.

'We'll pull him back in and interview him at the station. That might put the fear of God into him. Did he tell you any more?'

Helen shook her head. 'But he made a sort of veiled threat. Told me to watch myself, and that the play shouldn't be performed again. Then I got this. It arrived a few minutes after he'd gone, so I guess he could have sent it himself.'

She showed Sarah the photograph. 'I was trying to work out where it was taken from. I think either the cathedral gatehouse, or the shop doorway next to it. But I didn't see anyone. This was taken early this morning, before we found the body.'

Sarah looked at the image, then took off her glasses and rubbed her eyes. 'There should be CCTV of the gatehouse. That might have caught them. You didn't know you were being watched?'

'Nope.' She'd been absorbed in her own thoughts of the performance, Helen remembered. If someone had wanted to harm her, to do to her what had been done to William, they would have had plenty of opportunity. 'Have you found anything in the cathedral? Anything to say if Alice was there too?' she asked.

The policewoman shook her head. 'We're still searching. It's a massive place, as you'll appreciate. We think Mr Danbury may have been held in the old Water Tower, near the choir. We found a wallet there, which seems to have belonged to the victim.'

'What about the library? Have you looked there?' Helen thought of the play's epilogue, hidden by William Danbury among the cathedral's records. If whoever had killed him had attempted to get him to reveal the secret, might they have taken him there first?

'I don't know. I expect so. Why do you ask?'

'Oh...' Helen tailed off. 'I remembered they had a library. Lots of secrets in libraries.'

Sarah gave her a hard stare. 'If you think you know something...'

'It's just an idea. Maybe I could go and take a look?'

Sarah sighed. 'I really shouldn't let you. But all right. As long as the search team has already been through there, and you tell me immediately if you find anything interesting.'

Helen sped around the cathedral close. The library was on the far side of the cathedral, next to the cloisters. She tapped on the door.

'Oh! Hello again.' It was Canon Bryce. Of course it was; where else would she find the canon librarian but in the library?

'Have the police searched in here? Can I come and have a look?' she asked.

'They've had a quick look around. Why, what are you after?' He seemed reluctant to let her in.

'Just an idea.' She paused. There wasn't an obvious way to explain why she thought William might have hidden a document in the library without giving away what it was about. 'Did they tell you about Alice Delamare? She's William Danbury's neighbour, up at Harbledown. And I know she's interested in the history of the cathedral, so I thought she might come here sometimes.'

He frowned. 'Yes, I've known Alice for years. What about her?'

'She's missing. Since yesterday afternoon, and it looks like she might have been going to meet William. They had tickets for the theatre, under his name.'

He covered his mouth with his hands. 'Oh, no.' He took a step back, steadied himself on the door jamb. 'Not Alice.' He beckoned Helen in to the oak-panelled room with its rows of leather-bound books. 'What time?' he asked.

'The theatre? It was half past seven start, but…'

'No, what time was she last seen?'

'I don't know, exactly. Someone in Harbledown saw her going to get the bus. I expect they'll be checking the CCTV and so on.'

'She was here,' he interrupted. 'In the cathedral close.' He raised his eyes to the high ceiling, remembering. 'Around quarter past five. I'd just locked up the library for the night. I was going down for Evensong.' He sat on one of the tables, between the big microfiche machines. 'I saw her in the main cloister. It was raining and she asked if the Chapter House was still open.'

'The Chapter House?'

'Yes, I thought it was a bit odd. But she didn't tell me why. She seemed to be in a hurry. She said she was going to the theatre afterwards.'

'I see. We should tell the police. They're trying to find her.'

'Of course.' Canon Bryce looked anguished. 'I don't like this,' he said. 'Something is horribly wrong.'

Helen was puzzled. This was the man who had reacted with

calm to the discovery of William Danbury's corpse; who'd chatted with the boy from the choir and made coffee while they waited for the police. He seemed far more upset now than he had been this morning.

He jumped to his feet. 'Let's check the Chapter House,' he said.

They hurried through the cloister, under the fan-vaulted roof. Had she not been so anxious, Helen would have loved to stop and stare upwards at the colourful shields and carved bosses that adorned the ceiling.

'She was heading this way, along the south pane.' He pointed to the adjacent side of the cloister, in the shadow of the cathedral nave. 'I'd just locked up, like I said, so I was walking towards the door by the Martyrdom. I met her at the corner.'

'So would she have come through the cathedral?'

'Not necessarily. You can walk around the side and go straight into the cloister,' he said. 'Now,' he paused by a stone archway, dark oak doors closed, 'here we are.'

He opened the double doors, and another set of modern glass doors within them. Helen stepped inside, under the magnificently ornate carved ceiling. The Chapter House was far bigger than she'd anticipated, a huge hall with stone benches all along the sides and impressive stained-glass windows. At one end of the hall was a marble throne.

She heard the heavy oak door close behind her, and turned.

'Right, Helen,' said Canon Bryce. 'I think we should have a serious conversation. What do you know about the burial place of Thomas Becket?'

CHAPTER FIFTEEN

H elen stared at the man. His thin face, gaunt above his white collar and black gown, had no trace of a smile.

Not again, she thought.

She ran to the far end of the room and jumped onto the stone bench. Height was an advantage. She wasn't going to waste time trying to persuade another priest that she knew nothing of Thomas Becket's grave.

She scanned the room. To her right was a set of wooden steps, leading up to a small studded oak door. She began to move towards them.

'Helen. Please. It's important,' Canon Bryce said. He hadn't moved, standing still by the entrance door.

She reached the steps. Get out, find the police. Tell Sarah Greenley, let her deal with this. Don't get trapped.

He sighed. 'That door's locked. It leads out to the green court. It's always locked.'

She went up the steps, all the same, turned the iron handle and pushed hard. It didn't move. Right, then. She took a deep breath, braced one foot against the stairwell and set her shoulder to the door.

'Stop it. Don't be silly.' Canon Bryce flung the entrance doors open again. 'I'm not going to stop you from leaving. I want to find out what's happened to Alice. I thought we should work together. Privately.'

Helen hesitated. 'DCI Greenley knows I went to the library. She'll be looking for me.'

'I expect she will. She seems a very competent woman. Let's talk honestly. I looked you up, after this morning. You're the researcher who found the Marlowe play, aren't you? So you must know about the epilogue.'

Helen said nothing.

'William brought it to me,' he said. 'The epilogue. We found an appropriate place for it, in the library.'

'I see.' Helen relaxed very slightly. If Bryce was telling the truth, then William had trusted him. But perhaps, she thought, he shouldn't have done.

'It's gone. I've been searching all morning.'

'What?' Even Helen had not been told of the exact location of the epilogue. She had begged William not to destroy it, although it lacked the literary merit of the rest of the play. So little remained of Christopher Marlowe's life. There was only one verified manuscript of his plays, and every page was precious.

'After the police had taken our statements this morning, I went straight to the library. I knew his murder must have been something to do with Saint Thomas. The way his body was placed, where the tomb once stood…'

He broke off, rubbed his face. 'It's not there.' He walked to the stone bench and sat down, hunched over. 'I thought you might know where it is.'

Helen walked slowly down the steps and around the stone seating. She stood behind him for a moment. He didn't look round.

'No,' she said. 'But you're right, I found it. Francis Nash had the epilogue with him when he died.'

'That's what William said.'

She sat down next to him. 'Have you read it? The epilogue, I mean.'

'No.' The man looked sad. 'William said the fewer people who knew of it, the better. He didn't even tell me what was in it.' He paused. 'Do you have a copy?'

Helen wasn't sure yet whether to trust him.

'A transcript was made when it was discovered.' She had copied it into Richard's notebook in the study at Cobham Hall. That notebook was her single most precious possession. 'Who else knows?' she asked.

'That it's missing? Nobody. Just us.'

'About the epilogue. What it tells us.' If the canon librarian knows, she thought, who else?

'Oh, I see.' He paused for a moment. 'Nobody else has seen the epilogue. The dean approved the plan to keep the document here, safe and unlikely to be found accidentally. He didn't know where exactly it was hidden.'

'The archbishop?'

The man smiled for the first time. 'The boss? No need to bother him with the details. He leaves the business of the cathedral to the dean and chapter. Although we will have to brief him on recent events.'

So William and Alice were the only people who knew the secret revealed in the epilogue. Apart from herself, of course. If William and Canon Bryce were the only ones who knew where it was hidden – and Canon Bryce said it was missing – then surely William must have hidden it himself.

'When did you last see William?' she asked.

'Tuesday,' he said. 'I suppose he must have moved it then. He came in early, wanted some papers relating to the Victorian history of Eastbridge. I had to go down to the basement for them. Perhaps he wanted to distract me.'

Helen mused a moment. Why did William decide to move the epilogue from its hiding place two days before the play's first performance? And did he tell anyone else about his plans? Alice, for example.

She got up, paced the length of the hall. 'If Alice came here yesterday – what time did you say? Quarter past five?'

He nodded.

'Who else was around? Who would have seen her coming in? What if she'd left by that door at the back?' She ran to the door, not waiting for answers. 'Can you open it?'

He took out a big bunch of keys. 'I think so.' He clicked through the keys, then fitted one to the lock and pushed the door open.

They emerged onto a walkway, covered like the cloisters with a whitewashed vaulted roof. Beyond the stone pillars was a green lawn and a herb garden.

'This connects the back of the Chapter House to the archives, up that way,' said Canon Bryce, pointing. 'And over there are the dean's stairs to the cathedral, and the wheelchair lift to the crypt.'

'Wait.' Helen dropped to her knees. 'Look.' In the doorway, partly wedged beneath the half-open door, silver glinted. Helen pushed the door further open.

'It's a locket. A silver locket, like the one Alice wore.' She reached out a hand, then stopped herself. 'Quick. Go and find the police. This might mean she was here, and that she came out this way. We'd better not go any further, in case we mess up footprints and so on.'

'Of course.' Canon Bryce turned and hurried back through the Chapter House.

CHAPTER SIXTEEN

Sarah Greenley was furious that Helen had found the locket where her officers had missed it. She turned Helen and the canon out of the Chapter House, shouting brisk orders at scene of crime officers, who swapped grimaces with the search team, no doubt anticipating a dressing-down later.

'Dozy bunch,' she muttered to Helen, ten minutes later. 'I should have stayed with the Met. I'll find out who searched this room.'

Helen would not like to have been that person.

'Did you open it?' she asked.

The policewoman nodded. 'Yes. Do you know what was in it, then?'

'I don't. A photograph of her late husband?'

Sarah gave a grim smile. 'Nope. A bit of red thread, coiled up. What do you make of that?'

Helen shook her head. 'No idea.'

'Well, let me know if you think of something.'

Helen walked back to the library with Canon Bryce.

'Where have you been looking?' asked Helen. 'For the epilogue, I mean. Could it be somewhere else in the library?'

He hesitated. 'It's possible, of course. I've searched the

document boxes in that section of the archive. William chose the place. It was with the records of the Royal East Kent Regiment, the Buffs. He served with them, you know.'

'Of course.' Helen smiled, remembering William's military bearing and clipped neatness. 'Could I have a look? I'm quite good with archives.'

Helen sat on a wooden desk while Canon Bryce brought out big cardboard boxes of documents.

'It was supposed to be in this one,' he said, thumping a box down on the desk next to her. 'In one of these big envelopes. They're mostly old soldiers' reminiscences of campaigns and academic studies of the regiment. He'd labelled it "Master of Arts Dissertation by W H Danbury: The bureaucracy of amalgamation of the Kent regiments in the 1960s and 1970s". He thought that would be off-putting enough that no-one would bother to read it.'

Helen found herself laughing, despite the seriousness of their search. 'Very good. And the whole envelope has gone?'

Canon Bryce nodded. 'But you're welcome to have another look.'

Helen leafed through the white envelopes, checking the contents against the catalogue. She couldn't do the forensic work that the police were doing, but if William had hidden the epilogue, it seemed reasonable to assume that whoever had murdered him would be looking for it. Which meant she should try to find it first.

She shook out a bunch of cuttings from faded newspapers, all relating to the regiment's exploits in Aden in the 1950s. One caught her eye.

'What's this? It's out of place,' she said. She smoothed out a more recent newspaper cutting, dated 1997.

'Scholars gather for fifty-year inspection of archbishop's memorial,' the headline read, with a photograph of a group of men standing around an ornate tomb. 'What's that about?'

'Hmm?' He put on his glasses for a closer look. 'Oh, it's Archbishop Chichele. He founded All Souls College in Oxford in the fifteenth century. There's a tradition that they come to inspect the condition of the tomb every fifty years. I'm not sure why the cutting is in that folder, though. It must have been misfiled.'

'Maybe.' Helen read the cutting and set it down. 'I think I should take a look at the archbishop's tomb, though. Just in case. Can you show me?'

They entered the cathedral from the cloisters. There was no police guard on the door now. Sarah Greenley, under pressure from the cathedral authorities, had opened up the main body of the building with only the crypt off-limits as a crime scene.

Just inside the cathedral, they passed the striking sculpture of jagged swords, which marked the point where Thomas Becket had been struck down. Helen paused. This corner of the cathedral, this passageway, had been where it had all begun. She noticed Canon Bryce bow his head.

'The Martyrdom transept,' he said, his voice low. 'The Altar of the Sword's Point was set up here, after the murder. People came to venerate the tip of the sword, which broke off when Saint Thomas was killed.'

Helen grimaced. She didn't understand the religious enthusiasm for venerating weapons of murder. She looked again at the swords on the wall and realised they represented crosses. Another weapon, a method of torture and execution, sanctified and worshipped around the world.

She followed the canon up the steps to the quire, past the

gleaming mahogany stalls with their red cushions. To her left, she saw blue and white police tape across a plywood barrier, a padlock locking it closed.

'What's that?' she asked.

'It's the passageway through to the Water Tower. It's closed for restoration work. I don't know why the police have blocked it off, though.'

Helen paused. William may have been held in the Water Tower, Sarah Greenley had said. Right by the quire of the cathedral, where the choirboys sang. Had Alice, too, been brought here from the back door of the Chapter House?

'Here. Archbishop Chichele.'

Canon Bryce stood beside a brightly painted tomb, rich with red, blue and gold. An effigy lay on the tomb, clothed in crimson with his hands together in prayer, his mitred head resting on a golden cushion.

'It's certainly impressive,' said Helen. She stepped back to admire the pillars, intricately decorated and painted with figures of saints and kings, and the gilded canopy adorned with coats of arms.

'Look underneath,' said Canon Bryce.

She stooped to see the tomb's lower level.

'Oh. And that's rather gruesome,' she said. 'What's that about?'

Below the splendidly vested image of the archbishop was another figure. It was the same man, but stripped of his ecclesiastical robes, gaunt and naked, the only colour that of the pale stone. A corpse.

'It's a memento mori tomb, designed to remind us where we all go, no matter how important in life,' said Canon Bryce.

The protruding ribs and bony jaw reminded Helen only too

powerfully of their discovery of William that morning. She crouched down to see more closely.

'Archbishop Chichele had it made almost twenty years before his death,' said Canon Bryce. He pointed across the choir to a stone seat. 'That's the archbishop's chair, right opposite. He would have seen his tomb every day as he came to celebrate mass.'

What a weird religion, thought Helen. Meditating on death was one thing, but she had no desire to think about what she might look like as a corpse.

'Which reminds me, I'm supposed to be getting ready for Evensong. I'll need to leave you, Helen. Are you all right to see yourself out?' he asked.

Helen checked the time. Almost a quarter past five. A whole day since Alice had last been seen, and Helen was no closer to finding out what had happened to her. But something about this tomb – perhaps its echo of William's death – held her here.

'I'm fine,' she said. 'Thank you.'

He hurried away. Helen dropped to her haunches, gazed at the stone corpse. What did you bring me here for, William? Why did you put that cutting in the file, in place of the epilogue? On impulse, she reached through the railings to touch the finely carved cold hand.

And then she saw it. A scroll of paper, rolled small and tied with red thread, pushed beneath the curved hand of the cadaver.

She looked around quickly. No-one was in sight. She reached in and delicately removed the scroll. Resisting the temptation to open it immediately, she headed out of the quire, up a set of shallow steps worn into soft shelving curves. The pilgrim steps: the steps that pilgrims had walked up for hundreds of years on their way to see Becket's magnificent tomb.

Helen stopped at the top of the steps by the candle that burned, year-round, on the pavement of marble. It marked the spot where the tomb had stood, before its destruction by Henry VIII's men. Beneath a stained-glass window depicting the saint at prayer, she carefully untied the neatly knotted crimson thread and wound it around her finger. She unrolled the paper.

The lines were written in black ballpoint pen, the script neat with small letters.

'The Master protects the secret from beyond the tomb,' read the message. 'Studious in death, as he was in life: *per aspera ad cathedra.*'

The master. One of the masters of Eastbridge, then. A long line of men, chosen to oversee the charitable foundation of Eastbridge Hospital, and later to protect the secret of Becket's grave. A line which ended with William Danbury himself.

Helen gazed down the length of the cathedral, with its ornate tombs lining the walls and chapels. Beyond the tomb? Or – perhaps – within a tomb. Another tomb. The tomb of a master of Eastbridge?

She thought with despair of the list of masters, dating back in unbroken records to the twelfth century. Would she have to go through each one, find out where they were buried? It could take days.

She turned to the Latin, wishing for the hundredth time she had learned the language at school. But some of this was familiar, and she had picked up plenty of phrases during her literary studies. *Per aspera* – through aspiration, or struggle. The usual phrase was *ad astra per aspera* – to the stars through struggle. And *ad cathedra* – to the chair, or position. A cathedral was the seat of a bishop. Did William mean a master of Eastbridge who had also been Archbishop of Canterbury? Helen couldn't think of one. But then, perhaps he simply meant the cathedral.

How many of the masters of Eastbridge were buried here? Among the archbishops and saints, kings and princes, nobility and churchmen. She supposed Canon Bryce might know. She could ask him, after Evensong.

As the thought came into her head, she heard the first notes of the choir. She turned and walked down the steps, back into the body of the cathedral. The small congregation, a collection of mainly grey-haired respectable-looking people, sat in the nave. Purple-robed choirboys walked in procession, pure high notes raising goosebumps. Josh, the boy who had sung in the theatre, was among them, second from last. He was the only black chorister, she noticed. How did that feel? She thought of her own schooldays, the way she'd been teased for her height and for being the head teacher's daughter. She hoped Josh didn't get bullied.

Canon Bryce stood by the altar with the other clergy, one woman and one man, as the boys processed past and arranged themselves on the steps.

Helen felt the tension in her shoulders ease as the music dropped its notes of quiet peace. For a moment, the horror of William's death and the dread of Alice's disappearance stilled. She walked silently into the nave, keeping unobtrusively out of the light, and took a seat at the back of the congregation. She could think while she listened. And then she could quiz Canon Bryce when the service was over.

Quietly, she unwound the crimson thread from her finger. It

was smooth to the touch, silky. Embroidery silk, she supposed. She wound it into a skein, remembering what DI Greenley had said about Alice's locket. A coiled-up bit of thread. Like this one? she wondered.

CHAPTER SEVENTEEN

J osh was desperate to go down to the crypt. The choir had been told it was strictly out of bounds. No-one had told them why, but it hadn't taken long to find out.

He'd known something exciting was happening from the moment the police van had arrived in the close, while they were getting onto the minibus to school. And then Canon Derek had pretended nothing was the matter, when it obviously was. The woman from the theatre had been with him, and she'd looked really upset, like someone had died. Then at break time, Finlay saw on his phone that a dead body had been found in the cathedral.

Finlay said it was most likely Satanists conducting ritual sacrifices, and Ben said no, it was probably just some old person who got left behind after a service and died of old age. None of the teachers would tell them anything. They just put on serious faces and said it was very sad.

As soon as they'd got off the bus after school, Josh had gone to see Trey, one of the postern gatekeepers. Trey was his favourite person among the cathedral staff: a big man who liked to hear his stories of life in the choir.

'It was murder,' the man had reported, solemnly. 'The police have been here all day. The whole cathedral was closed this morning. The coroner's van came in this way, then I saw them wheel the body out on a trolley.'

Maybe Finlay was right, thought Josh. 'Was it Satanists?' he asked, trying to sound knowledgeable.

Trey laughed, a big laugh that shook his belly. 'What are you talking about? Satanists? What do you know about that stuff?'

Josh shrugged. 'All right. How did they kill him, then?'

Trey looked worried. 'You don't need to know that,' he said.

'I really do. Please, Trey. Go on.'

The big man looked around to see they were alone. 'Don't tell anyone I told you, then. He had his throat cut. Right across.' He drew his finger across his neck.

Josh swallowed, imagining the cold knife on his skin. He had friends who'd been stabbed. Well, maybe not friends, but he knew them: kids on his estate. One of his sister's friends' brothers was in a gang. He'd been knifed in the leg, and he'd vowed to shank the boy who did it. That was one of the reasons his mum had been so glad when Josh got the scholarship. No-one gets stabbed in Canterbury Cathedral, she'd told his dad. Let him go. He hoped she wouldn't hear about this.

'That's sick,' he said. Then he ran back to Choir House to tell the boys.

Ben was due to perform at the theatre that night, so he wasn't at Evensong. Josh and Finlay nudged each other as they walked through the cathedral and past the steps to the crypt. Fin rolled his eyes back in his head and drew his finger across his throat, earning them a furious stare from the choirmaster.

As they settled in position on the steps, Josh saw the woman from the theatre, sitting behind all the regular old people. She looked out of place, with her spiky short hair that made her look like a man, and her black jumper and jeans. He wondered what she was doing there.

He remembered her face that morning, when he'd seen her with Canon Derek. She'd tried to sound normal, but she'd looked awful, like she might faint. Had she actually seen the body? She'd had something on her hands. Had it been blood?

'Josh!' Fin nudged him. He'd missed his cue. Quickly, he found his place and started singing, darting an apologetic glance at the choirmaster. They were going to be in big trouble later. His usual ease with the music deserted him. His voice sounded off. He wasn't out of tune, but he couldn't slip into the flow of the notes. It was as if they no longer made sense, a collection of random sounds. He knew the boys around him would notice his blunders, and felt hot with shame. What was wrong with him?

As they stood for the blessing at the end of the service, he watched the woman. She stood like the rest of them, but didn't bow her head or mouth 'Amen'. Josh wondered again what she was there for. Maybe she just liked the singing. He wished it had been better. He didn't want her to think the choir was rubbish.

They processed out along the south transept, heading for the exit. Annoyed with himself for his mistakes, Josh longed to get outside, an hour of rec under the Oaks before tea.

'Wait,' said the choirmaster, looking grim. 'Joshua and Finlay. I want a word.'

They swapped worried glances as the other boys ran off into the evening sunshine.

'I know you're both feeling very special right now,' he said. 'It's exciting, performing at the theatre. But this is an extra. A privilege. Your job is here, in the cathedral. If you can't do that properly, I'll have to tell the theatre director that he'll need to find his soloists elsewhere.'

'But they couldn't do that in time…' began Finlay.

'Quiet. Finlay Robinson, if I ever see you behave like that in the cathedral again, I will have to consider whether you are fit to be a member of this choir.'

Fin stiffened in horror. 'I'm sorry.' His voice was small and scared.

'That's better. Now, straight back to Choir House. Go to your room. I don't want to see you again until dinner. Is that clear?'

Finlay nodded and escaped.

The choirmaster sighed. 'Joshua, where was your head tonight? Are you too tired? Should we pull you out of the play?'

'No!' Josh gasped. 'I'm sorry. I was thinking… about everything. About the man in the crypt. I wasn't concentrating properly. But I can do it, honest. I'll pay more attention.'

The choirmaster nodded. 'You did well last night. But you have to keep the standard. You can't have an off day, let yourself get distracted.' He hesitated. 'What do you know about the man in the crypt? What are the boys saying?'

'That he was dead,' said Josh, cautiously.

'What else?'

Josh thought of Trey. He didn't want to get him in trouble.

'It said on the news that the man was knifed,' he said. 'Some of the boys suspect the involvement of Satanists.'

Josh saw the man's lips twitch in what looked like the start of a smile, before he caught himself.

'There's no reason to think that,' he said, firmly. 'Best not to speculate. Don't spread rumours, Josh. Now, get an early night tonight. You're performing again on Sunday, aren't you?

Make sure you get plenty of rest.'

He strode away, across the close. Josh's shoulders sagged in relief. He'd got off lightly.

'Hello again, Josh.'

The woman was standing to one side of the exit, hanging back from the rest of the congregation as they chatted in the transept. He tried to remember her name. She seemed to guess and reminded him.

'Helen. We met after the show last night.' And this morning, he thought, when you'd just seen a dead body.

'Hullo. What are you doing here?'

She smiled. 'Good question. I wanted a word with Canon Bryce, but it looks like he's busy.'

Josh followed her gaze to where the tall man stood, surrounded by chatty congregants, probably all asking about the murder in the crypt.

'Can I help?' he asked, to be polite.

She tipped her head to one side. 'I don't know. I'm looking for a tomb. Someone who might be buried in the cathedral, who was once a master of Eastbridge Hospital.'

Josh didn't know what that was, but he hated admitting ignorance. And he liked the way the woman talked to him, as if he was another adult.

'What for?'

She eyed him for a moment, as if she wasn't sure whether she wanted to answer.

'It's a sort of treasure hunt. I think someone has hidden something in the cathedral. To do with the play,' she said.

'OK.' He liked the sound of that. 'Lots of people buried in the cathedral are archbishops,' he said, hoping he sounded knowledgeable. 'And deans. There's a whole chapel full of deans.'

They'd had a tour of the cathedral and its monuments when he first joined the choir. He wasn't particularly interested in history, but he liked the tombs with skeletons on them. There was a brilliant one in the Deans' Chapel, covered in bones and skulls. The choirboys sometimes talked about getting into the cathedral at night and opening them up, having a look at the bodies.

'Deans. What's the difference between a dean and an archbishop?' asked the woman.

'Really? You don't know?' Josh smiled, glad there was something he knew more about. 'The dean is in charge of the cathedral. He lives here and runs everything in Canterbury. The archbishop is in charge of the whole Church of England and he lives in London. We don't often see him here.' Josh had only met him once, at a big memorial service. He'd been friendly, singled Josh out of the choir and asked him about school.

'I see.' Helen was chewing her lip, looking thoughtful. 'You've reminded me of something. Thanks, Josh. I think I need to look someone up. You've been really helpful.'

'Can't we look for the tomb now?' he asked.

She looked at Canon Derek, still surrounded by people. 'All right. Do you know this one? Dr John Boys, dean of the Cathedral in – let me think – it would have been the early seventeenth century. He was a master of Eastbridge.'

Josh didn't know. It might be fun to look for it, though.

'I think we should start with the Deans' Chapel,' he said. 'It's over the other side.'

CHAPTER EIGHTEEN

D r John Boys. Of course, thought Helen. Not only had the churchman been a former master of Eastbridge, but he'd been involved in the successful effort to suppress the Becket play when it resurfaced after Christopher Marlowe's death. And he'd been appointed as dean of Canterbury Cathedral towards the end of his life.

As she followed the serious little choirboy across the cathedral, Helen tried to remember what she knew of Boys. Like Christopher Marlowe, he had been a pupil at the Kings School in Canterbury, within the cathedral grounds. Boys had also gone on to Cambridge University, but instead of plunging into the raffish life of the playhouse, he'd had a distinguished career in the church.

Helen saw him as Marlowe's alter ego, the boy who had done what was expected of a successful scholarship lad in Elizabethan times. He'd been ten years younger than the playwright, arriving at Cambridge around the time that Marlowe met his premature death. As if warned by Marlowe's downfall, Boys had studied dutifully, then worked his way through a succession of Kentish vicarages, picking up honorary positions such as Eastbridge along the way, before being rewarded with the hugely important role of dean of Canterbury Cathedral.

'Almost there.' The boy led her across the nave to the Martyrdom transept, then through a gothic arch into a side chapel with soaring high windows and fine fan vaulting. 'Look at this one.' Josh pointed to a gruesome marble tomb decorated – if that was the word – with sculpted skulls and bones. Ribcages, half a pelvis and assorted leg bones provided a graphic reminder of the fate that awaited the bodies in the tombs. And those of us still walking around, thought Helen.

'It's amazing. Creepy, though.' Helen checked the name on the tomb, then stepped back to scan the room.

'Do you think that's what the bones look like inside?'

'Maybe.' Helen didn't want to think about what the tomb looked like inside. She'd seen more than enough dead bodies today already.

The next tomb along was a grander affair altogether. Pink marble columns flanked a fine carving of a man in an Elizabethan ruff and church robes, seated at a table before a wall lined with books. The man rested his head on his hand, as if weary of the book propped up at the table before him.

Studious in death as he was in life… Helen's skin prickled. *Per aspera ad cathedra*. Through a life of striving to a seat in the cathedral. This must be it. She checked the inscription: Dr John Boys.

He'd been interred in the biggest, most impressive tomb in the Deans' Chapel, a few steps away from where Thomas Becket had met his death. She studied Boys's pious marble face, the eyes blank. What was his legacy? The suppression of a play.

She thought of the contrast with Christopher Marlowe's unmarked resting place, somewhere in a scruffy churchyard in Deptford. His murdered body tumbled into a pit with victims of the plague. If one of the two Canterbury scholars deserved a marble monument, surely the playwright did, too.

'Is this the right one? Why are you interested in it?' asked Josh. She'd forgotten he was there. She'd probably told him more than she should already, but he had been so keen to help.

'Yeah, that's the one.' She hesitated. Now she was here, she needed to examine it, look for the hidden epilogue. But she couldn't do that under Josh's beady eyes.

'Thanks, you've been really helpful. Can you do something else for me? Check whether Canon Bryce is still talking to people?'

'Did you see the man's body this morning? Had his throat really been cut?' asked the boy. It was a quid pro quo, Helen realised. He'd help her, but he wanted to know what she knew.

'I saw him,' she said. 'But I don't know what had happened to him. I'm not a doctor.'

'Bet there was a lot of blood, though, wasn't there?'

She sighed. 'There was.'

'And,' Josh drew nearer, dropped into a whisper, 'was it Satanists? Finlay thinks it was.'

'No,' she said, firmly. 'There's no reason to think that at all.'

Seemingly satisfied, he ran off. Helen stepped up behind the altar rail and drew closer to the tomb. A pair of griffins held the dean's book support. Helen pushed up onto tiptoes to see if any document had been placed on top of the support. She smiled slightly, imagining the dean turning away from Marlowe's epilogue in disgust. But there was nothing.

She stepped back, looked under his marble chair. Nothing. She turned to the table that held the book support. Curiously, there was a real crimson velvet cushion underneath, set on the marble floor. Helen slid her hand underneath the cushion.

Nothing. She turned it over. The smooth velvet had been cut, a rough slit along the side.

She reached inside, felt around among the feathers.

'What are you doing?' Josh stood at the archway into the chapel, his voice accusatory.

Helen jumped. 'I thought you'd gone to see Canon Bryce,' she said.

'He did.' The canon stood behind Josh, his tall figure severe in silhouette. 'I thought I should come and see what you were up to.'

'I was going to tell you,' said Helen. Her earlier unease about the man resurfaced. 'You were busy with the service. And Josh here was able to show me John Boys's tomb.'

Canon Bryce walked into the chapel and sat on one of the wooden chairs.

'Better be getting back now, Joshua. It's almost time for dinner.' Unwillingly, the boy backed out of the chapel.

'When I left you, you were contemplating Archbishop Chichele's tomb,' said Canon Bryce. 'Did you find something there?'

Helen nodded. 'A note. I don't know William Danbury's handwriting, but I guessed it could be from him. It referenced this tomb. John Boys.'

'Indeed. And what are you doing with that cushion?'

Helen took it from the tomb and put it down on the chair next to him. 'Look. It's been cut open.'

He picked it up, inspected it. 'You thought William Danbury might have hidden the epilogue in here?'

'Well, it's a possibility,' Helen said.

The churchman turned the cushion over and looked at the rip. Suddenly, he seemed to lose patience, tearing it open with a cry of frustration and shaking out the feathers. The chapel filled with them, white curls flying into the air, a blizzard that whirled around their heads, then settled softly.

'Canon Bryce…'

'It's not there.' He stood grim-faced, feathers landing on his black-clad shoulders, then turned and strode away, the empty cushion case clutched in his hand.

Helen watched him go, her heart beating hard. His burst of violence had unsettled her. That was not normal behaviour.

His figure receded, feathers eddying on the stone floor in his wake, until he swept out of the door by the Martyrdom. She wondered what the ladies on the cleaning rota would make of all the feathers. Although, she supposed, they would probably be more concerned at having to scrub away the blood from the crypt.

She sat back down on the wooden chair and unclenched her fists. In her left hand was the small roll of paper she had found when she put her fingers through the slit in the velvet cushion.

She started to untie the crimson thread.

'What does it say?'

Josh had materialised again, rounding the chapel entrance, eyes big.

Helen smiled, despite herself. 'Did you hear all that?'

He nodded. 'Canon Derek seems a bit cross,' he said, coming to sit next to her. 'Don't you think he's acting strangely? Like this morning, when he pretended there was nothing wrong. Was he with you when you saw the body?'

Helen regarded the eager face. 'I'm not going to tell you what we saw. The police need me to keep that secret. But yes, we found the body together.'

She was itching to read the paper, but all too conscious that this was not an innocent treasure hunt.

'I don't want you to get hurt, Josh,' she said. 'I'm not sure what's going on here, but it could be dangerous. Someone has died already. Why don't you go back to have your dinner? You've been really helpful. And I promise to tell you what I find out, once it's safe.'

He shook his head, looking mutinous. 'People always say they'll tell me things later,' he said. 'They think I'll get upset. But I don't. I just like to know what's happening.'

'What sort of things?' Helen asked, gently.

He kicked the floor. 'About my mum, mainly. My aunties say it's her nerves. But she gets depression,' he said.

'I'm sorry,' said Helen. 'That's tough.'

'One time, she took a load of pills. My sister found her and called the ambulance. People always say not to worry. But how can I not worry unless I know what's going on?'

He kicked the floor again. They sat in silence for a moment.

'Yeah,' said Helen. 'I think you've got a point.'

She started to unroll the paper.

'There you are. I've been looking for you.' Another boy burst into the chapel, his face flushed from running.

Josh looked up. 'What are you doing, Ben? You're supposed to be at the theatre. You'll be late,' he said.

The boy put his hands on his knees and doubled over, his shoulders heaving. 'Stitch,' he said. 'Ow.'

He straightened up, one hand clutching his side.

'The play's been cancelled. One of the actors was stabbed. They reckon he might die.'

Helen felt cold. No, she thought. Please don't let it be him.

'Which actor?' She got to her feet, holding onto the back of the wooden chair.

'The main one. Gregory Hall? Someone cut his throat.'

A flustered woman arrived, also out of breath. 'Joshua, Ben. Both of you need to get straight back to Choir House. We want everyone safely inside. Now.'

CHAPTER NINETEEN

There was a policeman standing at the stage door to the Marlowe Theatre, barring the way.

'Sorry, madam. Theatre's closed. Refunds round the front. No-one comes in this way,' he said.

Helen swallowed her frustration and rang Henry's mobile again. Again, it went to voicemail.

'Henry, I just heard about Greg. I'm so sorry. Can you call me when there's news?'

News. The thought of what that news might be dug a hollow in her chest. Could someone have their throat cut and survive? She tried to push down the image that kept rising in her mind's eye of the gaping mess where poor William's throat had been. No-one could have survived that.

She paced the riverside path, wondering what to do. She thought of Greg, his vitality and strength after the show; his kindness and concern that morning. She'd liked him, despite herself, almost. She'd feared he would be rather grand or conceited, but he hadn't been like that at all.

There were footsteps behind her. Nervous, Helen spun around, half-expecting to see the weaselly protestor from earlier. It was Charlie, the assistant director, auburn curls gleaming. Her face was white with strain. Helen saw with horror splashes of blood on her white trainers, lines of blood beneath her fingernails.

'Have you heard?' Charlie asked, her voice high and thin.

'Only just now. What's happened? Is he...?' Helen didn't want to say the word.

'He's lost a shed-load of blood. The paramedic told me that a minute later, he would have been dead. He's in hospital. It could go either way.'

'Jesus.' Helen took a long, shaky breath. 'What happened?'

'He was late and not answering his phone. I went over to the hotel to see what was going on. Sometimes he oversleeps.' Charlie stopped. 'I need to sit down.'

Helen took her arm and guided her to a bench. She sat beside her, remembering how only the previous night, the woman had done the same for her. But then, the blood had been fake.

The woman breathed deeply and began again, her voice more normal now. 'I have spare keys to all the actors' rooms, in case of oversleeping. Or over-partying, overdosing.' She shut her eyes. 'I've seen some pretty nasty sights in actors' hotel rooms, Helen. But nothing like that.'

Gregory Hall had been crouched on the floor, hands clutched to his neck, covered in blood.

'He was still conscious, trying to stop the bleeding. It just kept coming, running over his hands. He was... sort of gurgling.

'I yelled for help, grabbed a towel and did what I could. One of the cleaning staff heard me and rang the ambulance. Then we basically held his neck together until they got there.'

'Oh, my God. That's awful.' Helen tried again to banish the vision of William Danbury's ravaged body.

'Yeah. He lost consciousness while I was holding him. I could see the fear in his eyes, this frantic appeal. And then it sort of faded out. I thought he was dead, but the paramedics said not. They took him away. I talked to the police, then got changed and came back here. I didn't know what else to do.'

'Where's Henry? He must be frantic.'

'You bet. He's at the hospital now. The insurers are going apeshit and the actors are all terrified. I thought I should come back here and talk to them, but most of them have gone. Actually, most of them are on trains back home. No-one wants to be next. God knows what this means for the rest of the run. They're saying the play is cursed.'

Helen exhaled. 'Christ. What a mess.'

Cursed. Could it be? One performance of a play suppressed by the Church for four hundred years. And now one man was dead, another clinging to life, a woman missing. Every performance equals one dead body.

Helen thought of Christopher Marlowe, stabbed to death with his own dagger just days after completing the play. Of Walter Raleigh, who had intended to stage it, and was beheaded as a traitor. And, of course, Richard.

She looked up into the darkening sky. Helen didn't believe in curses. Evil came from all-too-human greed and cruelty. No need for supernatural explanations.

'It's not cursed,' she said, firmly. 'Greg was threatened by that bunch of idiot protestors. We need to find out who did this.'

Charlie smiled. 'Very logical,' she said. 'I'm afraid the theatrical world doesn't really think like that.'

No, thought Helen, but the police do. 'The hotel must have CCTV. They'll find him, surely.' Greg's attacker must have been covered in blood. How could they have escaped notice?

'Let's hope so.' Charlie got up and walked to the bridge. 'It's weird. When I went in, the receptionist said the driver I'd booked had gone up to Greg's room. I mean, I didn't book anything. But the guy, whoever he was, used my name.'

'That's odd.' Helen joined Charlie on the bridge. 'He must know you. Or about you.'

Helen thought again of the man who'd thrown fake blood. Charlie had taken charge, made the announcements and dealt with the police. Had he found out Charlie's name then? She tried to imagine him wielding a knife, slashing a throat.

'You didn't see anybody on your way to Greg's room?' she asked. 'I'm thinking about that protestor from last night. He was back again, hanging around here at lunchtime.'

She shook her head. 'I don't think so. I'd have remembered him, I reckon.' She was overtaken by a giant yawn. 'I'm whacked. I'm going to check again that there's no-one backstage, then I'm heading to my hotel for a shower. And to sit by the phone until Henry rings.'

'Of course.' Helen needed to decide where to go. She'd checked out of her expensive hotel – the hotel where Gregory Hall had been attacked – at lunchtime. She supposed she ought to go back to London. But how could she, with Greg's life in the balance and Alice still missing?

'Which hotel are you in?' she asked. 'I'd like to stick around for a while.'

As she checked into Charlie's budget hotel, Helen found the scroll of paper from John Boys's tomb in the pocket of her jeans. She'd completely forgotten about it. Upstairs in the clean but spartan room, she sat on the bed and unrolled it. It was short this time; just six words.

'No chickens, these brave guardian soldiers,' she read. She frowned, put it down. Chickens? What on earth did that mean?

God, more riddles. More clues to unravel and follow. Compared to the terrible news about Greg, the whole thing seemed childish, pointless. She tried to remember what Canon Bryce had told her in the library. William had been a military man, a member of a Kentish regiment. Were those the soldiers he meant?

She stared again at the paper. Why would William Danbury, who seemed a rather prosaic, logical sort of man, go to the trouble of setting up a trail of clues? If he wanted to hide the epilogue, surely he would just do that? He didn't want anyone to find it. The whole idea was that it would remain hidden.

She tried to imagine him, in his smart grey suit and tie, skipping around the cathedral slipping scraps of paper into tombs. Tying them up with crimson silk. And who did he think would discover the clues? Only Canon Bryce would have found the misplaced cutting – and even he had not picked up on its significance. He would know about the tombs, though. Were the clues aimed at him? But if so, why move the epilogue at all, if no-one else had known where it was originally?

She wished she could talk to Alice about it. Alice had known William better than anyone else, the warden at Harbledown had said. Helen thought again of the coil of thread in Alice's locket. How close were they? she wondered.

Perhaps the clues were for Alice. But why not just tell her? There was something unnecessarily theatrical about the whole thing. As if they were meant to distract her from something.

William had planned to see the play the previous night. He'd known about Helen's part in its discovery, and her promise that the epilogue would remain unperformed. He knew that she knew about Eastbridge's role in the suppression of the play. So would he guess that she knew about John Boys?

The more she thought about it, the more Helen began to feel that William Danbury had laid the trail specifically for her.

CHAPTER TWENTY

The man was back. Alice saw him walking through the meadow, the hood of his anorak pulled up over his face. His shoulders were slumped and he had a plastic bag in one hand. She watched him shamble towards the chapel and listened as he unlocked the padlock.

She'd guessed his age as mid-forties or thereabouts. The age that Jean's son would be now. Was it him? Alice hadn't had a good look at his face, yet. But who else would be helping Jean in this mad enterprise?

She tried and failed to remember Jean's son's name. She ought to know, after everything that had happened. He'd been a timid boy, big for his age, and rarely spoke. He kept his head ducked low as Jean and his sister argued. God, they argued. About everything, from whether the girl could get her ears pierced to what music she listened to, and her mother's political opinions.

Charlotte, that was it. Charlotte and… something else fancy. Something unexpected, for Jean.

She heard his heavy tread come up the steps. The door opened.

'Food,' he said, thrusting the plastic bag towards her.

'Thank you,' said Alice, walking to meet him. 'I was just

thinking about you.'

'Me?' He stared at her. That impassive face, heavy and stolid. Straight hair the colour of wet sand, plastered to his head. She had a flash of memory: the boy sitting at the kitchen table with a glass of milk, Mark trying to get him to talk. He'd eaten a packet of biscuits, looked frightened, and said nothing.

'You.' She looked at the bag of food dangling from his fist. On the back of his hand, a wonky tattoo in faded blue ink. She stared at the letters: OF + CF. It came to her.

Please, sir, can I have some more?

'Oliver. Isn't it?'

He looked wary, glancing around the room and down the stairs. 'I didn't say anything. Did she tell you?'

Alice forced herself to smile, as if he was still a nine-year-old boy, sitting under the table in the church hall, waiting for the meeting to finish.

'I remember you from Chatham. When your mum used to bring you and your sister along to parish meetings, because she didn't have a babysitter. I wondered what had happened to you. Don't you remember me?'

He shrugged. 'No. I was a kid.'

'You were.' Alice tried to remember anything about him, anything that he'd liked or been interested in. At one stage, she had tried to get her two boys to play with him, but they'd been chalk and cheese. But apart from the business with Derek...

Wait. Another memory, Derek Bryce taking all the children out canoeing, on the Chatham marina. And then, of course, Jean had used it against him.

'You used to go canoeing with the Sunday school, didn't you? My boys loved it; always came back soaked to the skin. Did you enjoy it?'

114

'Yeah.' A spark of interest, somewhere behind those dull eyes. How could she keep him talking? She would quickly run out of canoe-related chat. Could she make friends with him, maybe even get him to leave the door unlocked, or take a message to someone? It was a faint hope. She remembered the way he'd slung William around. And – she supposed – he would have been the one to kill William. She shivered. He wasn't that small boy any more.

'What about your sister?' she asked. 'Charlotte. I remember her very well.' CF, she thought, glancing again at the tattooed letters. Oliver Forbes and Charlotte Forbes. Alice wondered what had happened to the girl. Somehow, she doubted that she was still helping her mother out.

His face flushed red and he clenched his fists. Alice noticed splashes of something dark on his anorak sleeves and jeans.

'Shut up.' He dropped the bag of food, a plastic bottle of water rolling over the floorboards. Alice shrank back against the wall, feeling the rough edges of the flints.

Oliver stamped on the bag, then kicked the battered remains of a sandwich and an apple to the wall. He was shaking with rage.

'Don't talk about her. Just don't.' He loomed over her. There were flecks of blood on his face, in his hair. William's blood?

'Right. I'm sorry.'

He seized her jaw in one big hand, twisted her face so that her neck was at its furthest extension. His other hand pressed against her windpipe. Alice's breath stopped in her throat.

Oh God, she thought. God, remember me? Alice. You have William there. And Mark. I don't mind joining them, really I don't. I've had a good innings. But there is work still to do. Please. Help me get out of this one.

One more inch and her neck would snap. He brought his face close, his stale breath making her stomach clench. She tried to swallow.

'I'll kill you if you say her name again.'

Alice could say nothing. His clammy skin oozed sweat from open pores. His blue eyes, mean little pricks of light in his fleshy face, were fixed on hers. She had no doubt he meant every word. She tried to compose herself, resign herself to death. She must forgive him, let go of the anger and fear. It would soon be over, she told herself. And yet, she wasn't ready to go.

She heard footsteps running up the stairs.

'Drop.'

He let go. Alice fell back against the wall. She fought against dizziness, commanding her legs to hold her up. She wheezed, tried to get air back down her dry throat.

'Now, what is all this about?' Jean, her voice icy. 'I sent you to give our guest some food, not to strangle her.'

'Sorry,' he mumbled, head down, as if expecting a blow.

Jean paused. 'Good boy.' She placed a hand on his cheek, smiled. 'Look at me. That's better. Now, back to your room. Wait for me to call you. All right?'

He turned and walked from the room, shoulders slumped. Alice heard his steps recede down the stairs.

Gasping for breath, she slid down the wall and sat. What unlucky chance had made his sister's name a trigger for his fury?

'What happened? He doesn't usually kick off without provocation.'

Alice looked at the floor. It was wet, she noticed. God, had the water bottle split? She scrambled over to it and held it up, battered but intact. Thank goodness. She opened it, took a sip, then another, soothing her parched throat.

'I recognised him. From Saint Augustine's, when you used to bring them along to meetings. Oliver and Charlotte,' she said, cautiously. 'I was wondering what happened to them. I asked him about Charlotte.'

Jean nodded. 'I see. Well, Oliver is still with me. He's a good boy, mostly. His sister is not welcome. She left us, many years ago. They never got on. Best not to mention her,' she said. 'I won't always be here to protect you.'

Alice forced herself to smile. 'If you let me go, you won't need to be. I'll be able to look after myself.'

Jean pulled her coat closer around her body. 'We know that's not true. Look, you can't even feed yourself properly.' She smiled thinly at the food strewn around the floor.

Alice said nothing. She thought of the daughter, wondered what the story was. Charlotte had been a year or two older than Oliver and had taken after her father for looks. A small ginger-haired girl, awkward and angular in her early teens, skinny legs like lengths of knotted liquorice in her black school tights. She'd been sharp, clever, quarrelsome. Not, perhaps, the most comfortable sister for a quiet, shy boy with little academic ability. Certainly not a comfortable daughter for a woman like Jean.

'I came to warn you,' said Jean. 'One more night. I'm getting impatient, Alice. You could help me. Or you could wait until I don't need you any more.' She smiled, the same practised smile she'd used on Oliver.

'What will you do then?' asked Alice, touching the tender bruising around her jaw. 'Get Oliver to break my neck?'

Jean laughed her annoying laugh. 'Funny. But stupid,' she

117

said. She snatched the water bottle from Alice and poured it on the floor. 'There. A thirsty night to decide whether to help me or not. If I send my boy back, it means you've left it too late.'

She paused, looked at Alice with her head cocked to one side, waiting. Alice looked away.

'Right, then.' She walked from the room. Alice heard her lock the door, then her footsteps receded down the stairs. At the bottom, the rattle of the padlock.

Alice tried not to cry. Everything she did seemed to make things worse. She glanced at the crucifix on the wall, remembered her earlier plea.

Thank you, God. Thank you for giving me more time. And for giving me my daily bread, even if most of it is squashed.

She picked up a flattened triangle of sandwich, grated cheese smashed to a paste. Oh, well. She brushed it off and took a bite. The bread was wet. She forced herself to swallow it anyway. She needed strength. Would need strength, for whatever was to come.

She put her finger to the ground, touched the wet boards. There were little pools of water where Oliver had been standing. Wet footprints. From before Jean had poured the water away, not afterwards.

Why did Oliver have wet feet? And not just damp from walking through the grass after yesterday's rain, but actually wet, as if he'd been paddling in the sea.

Or in a river. Alice went to the window. The stream flowed beneath the chapel, around the eyot on which it sat. He must come and go by the water, she realised, avoiding the only access point from the street. She scanned the meadow, but there was no sign of him in the growing dusk.

Another night ahead. Alice sought out a dry patch of floor, up near the altar. The night before, she had found a pile of hassocks under the table and pulled them out to make a couch. No sense in being more uncomfortable than she had to be. She sat on one, piled another two up behind her to support her aching back.

She wondered if anyone had noticed her absence yet. The warden, perhaps? Terry, with his friendly smile, usually called around every other day. Eva, who lived on the other side of William, although she was getting a bit forgetful. Scatty.

Alice tried not to think about William's house, standing empty. Their two alms houses, next to each other, both silent and unpeopled. She sighed. She'd rarely been as happy anywhere as these past few years in Harbledown. The simple space, quick and easy to clean, suited her. It reminded her of the rooms she'd rented in Algeria as a young woman, travelling alone in north Africa. A place to eat, a place to sleep, a place to read and study. That's all she'd ever really needed.

She looked around the whitewashed chapel, picked up a piece of bruised apple. A place to sleep, a place to eat. What a pity she didn't have any books with her.

She checked the lectern. Of course. She took the big Bible from its stand and sat back down. Frowning in the dim light, she started to read.

CHAPTER TWENTY-ONE

Helen showered and wished she had some clean clothes to change into. She'd tried to scrub away the blood from the knee of her jeans, but the stain still showed, brownish now it had dried. Her white shirt from the night before was unwearable, soaked in fake blood.

I am in blood stepped in so far, that should I wade no more, returning were as tedious as go o'er. Superstitious actors refused to say the name of Shakespeare's *Macbeth*. The Scottish play, the cursed play. Was Marlowe's *Thomas Becket* also to be linked forever with a curse? Would it be known only as the Canterbury play, spoken of with a shudder? Blood at the opening night, blood in the cathedral crypt, blood pouring from the neck of the first man to play Marlowe's Becket.

She checked her phone again, hoping for an update on Greg's condition. The media were going completely mad about it. She noticed an urgent message from Nick, her journalist friend, asking her to call and tell him what the hell was going on. He was in New York, but was trying to arrange a flight back.

She allowed herself a moment's schadenfreude. She'd offered Nick a ticket for the previous night's performance, but he'd said he was too busy. She knew that Elizabethan drama wasn't exactly his thing, but had been disappointed, nonetheless. Bet he wished he'd been there now, she thought, deleting the message.

The phone rang. It was DCI Greenley's number.

'Sarah? Any news from the hospital?'

'No. Sorry. He's hanging on, though, so that's something. Where are you, Helen? Still in Canterbury?'

She named the hotel. 'I was about to go and find something to eat. I'm starving.'

'Me too.' The policewoman sounded awkward. 'Could you bear some company? I'm supposed to be off-duty, but I can't just sit around at home.'

Helen agreed. She didn't want to be alone, either.

'Great. I'll see you in the bar in fifteen minutes.'

Sarah was already at a table in the corner when Helen got there, a small glass of red wine and the menu propped up in front of her. She'd taken off her jacket and was wearing a soft green blouse, but still had 'police' written all over her. Her face relaxed into a smile.

'What can I get you? I think the lasagne looks safest of the food options.'

'Sounds fine. I'll have the same as you.' Helen sat. The plastic-topped table looked like it could do with a good wipe-down. She rubbed at it with a paper napkin.

Over their meal, Sarah filled her in on the police's progress.

'We've got CCTV from the hotel of the man who attacked Mr Hall. Big guy, six foot plus, dressed up like a chauffeur with a peaked cap. Unfortunately, that means the pictures don't show his face. There's something else, though. A tattoo on the back of his hand.'

'OK.' Helen thought for a moment. 'It doesn't sound like the guy who threatened me, then? The protestor.'

Sarah shook her head, chewed and swallowed. 'He's in custody, anyway. We brought him in after you reported him at lunchtime. Oh, and it wasn't him who sent you that photo. It was sent from Rochester, the digital analyst reckons. But he could have taken it and forwarded it on. There was no sim card in his phone when we pulled him in, which is more than a bit suspicious. He must have ditched it.

'He let one thing slip. He used the word "she" when referring to the organiser of the protest. Then he clammed up again. We have a membership list from Christianity in Crisis, from when Francis Nash was in charge. One of my PCs is going through it. I've told him to focus on the women. I don't suppose you remember any senior women from the group?'

'Sorry, I only met Father Nash and Lady Joan,' said Helen. She remembered Nash boasting that the organisation had tens of thousands of signed-up members. Finding just one would be a big job. 'Did you manage to trace the chauffeur once he left the hotel?'

Sarah looked annoyed. 'No. He went out the back of the hotel, then disappeared. We're still trawling the street CCTV, but I can't work out why we haven't picked him up again. We'll put the photos from the hotel out through the media. There's a press conference in a couple of hours. Not me, thank God. I've lined up one of our more photogenic inspectors to do it. We've got TV coming from literally all over the world.'

She stopped to chew her lasagne. 'What do you think's in this?' she asked. Helen, poking at the dubious-looking mince, was wondering the same thing. She took a swig of wine to cut through the grease.

'Did you find any more signs of Alice in the cathedral?' she asked. She thought of the little silver pendant, trodden into the doorway outside the Chapter House.

'More CCTV,' said Sarah. 'Thank God for the surveillance state.'

The pictures had shown a man in a hooded anorak, the same build as the attacker from the hotel, marching Alice out of the back of the Chapter House and up a set of stairs into the cathedral.

'We'd already found William's wallet in the Water Tower. It looks like Alice and William may have been held in there, before William was taken to the crypt and killed.

'Then we picked up something suspicious, around eleven o'clock at night. What looks like the same man rolling a trolley, one of those catering trolleys they use in hotels and restaurants. He bumped it down the dean's stairs, then across the cloisters. We think he went out the Mint Yard Gate. Which is usually locked, so he must have had a key. The cathedral constables are embarrassed not to have noticed this manoeuvre,' she said, voice deadpan. 'They thought it was someone from the restaurant in the cathedral lodge.'

'And then?' Helen had given up on the lasagne and was eating the garlic bread that had come with it. She wondered if a second glass of wine would be a bad idea.

'That's the annoying thing. We lose him again. There's a shot of him crossing Palace Street towards King Street, then he's gone.' Sarah pulled up her phone and showed Helen the map.

'King Street goes down to the theatre,' said Helen.

'Yeah, but we would have seen him come out the other end. There's a camera at the junction with The Friars. So he must have turned off somewhere.

'Down towards the river,' said Helen. 'The back of the hotel leads onto a street by the river, too.'

She had a sudden shiver of fear. Was that where Alice was, her body streaming with green weed, caught in the undergrowth?

'I know. We've looked already. I've put in a request for a diver search team. But it's shallow and clear; you wouldn't expect to need divers.'

Fast-flowing, though, Helen remembered, thinking of how the leaves had whipped past on the current.

'I wondered if you'd found anything else out,' said Sarah. 'I know you went poking round the cathedral. One of the constables was suspicious. A bit late for that, as I told him.'

Poor constable, thought Helen.

'I did, a bit,' she admitted. 'But I don't know that this is going to help much. It looks like William Danbury removed a document that had been kept in the library. He left some clues, though. I've been trying to find it.'

She took the second scroll of paper from her pocket and smoothed it on the table.

'What do you make of this?'

Sarah pulled out her reading glasses. 'Chickens? What's all that about?'

Helen shrugged. 'No idea. The soldiers might be something to do with William, though. He was in a local regiment.'

'OK.' Sarah had her phone out again. 'Which one?'

Helen shook her head. 'I'm trying to remember. Canon Bryce told me. Local, so the Kent Regiment, something like that?'

Sarah tapped it into her phone and laughed. 'There you go. That's your chickens.' She held the results out for Helen to see. 'The Royal East Kent Regiment, known as the Buffs.' She smiled at Helen's blank face. 'Buff Orpington. It's a famous breed of chicken, originally bred in Kent. I was going to start keeping them, now I've got a nice big garden. All part of my carefully planned quiet country life.'

Helen laughed. 'Chickens? You? Seriously?'

'Seriously. We could use the eggs.' DCI Greenley waved the waiter over and paid for their meal.

'Come on. Let's go.'

Helen drained her wine glass and got to her feet. Things seemed to be getting away from her again.

'Where are we going?'

'The Warriors' Chapel, in the cathedral. It's dedicated to the Buffs.'

CHAPTER TWENTY-TWO

E ven with DCI Greenley by her side, Helen felt there
was something spooky about exploring the cathedral
in the dark. The policewoman's pass got them through
the Christchurch Gate without questions, and a constable was
summoned to open the south-west door to the cathedral.

The last time she'd entered by this door, Helen had been with
Canon Bryce and they'd discovered the body in the crypt. She
hoped she wouldn't need to descend those steps again.

'What exactly are you looking for, ma'am?' asked the
constable. He looked nervous and treated Sarah with careful
respect. She must have been giving the cathedral police a hard
time.

'Take us to the Warriors' Chapel, please.' Sarah made the
request as if this was the obvious place to want to visit at nine
o'clock at night.

'This way.'

They walked down the aisle through the cathedral nave,
sharp oblongs of gold painted onto the floor from the floodlighting that came through the high windows. By contrast, the
inky dark of the shadows was fathomless. Helen felt as if she
might disappear at any moment, step into a patch of nothing
and plunge to infinity. She shivered. Anyone could be in those

shadows, watching.

The constable flicked on a torch, the beam sweeping across the fluted stone pillars. Their footsteps echoed loudly, sounding like the feet of more than three people. Helen glanced behind her, thinking of all the feet that had trodden this way before. Monks from medieval times, priests and choristers. Pilgrims in their hundreds of thousands, regular churchgoers, millions of tourists. And William Danbury, on his last journey through the cathedral.

The steps to the crypt were just ahead. Helen turned her eyes away from the staircase. The image of William's body, his head twisted around on what remained of his neck, was all too sharp. Her steps faltered.

'Helen?' Sarah was looking at her with concern.

'Sorry. Just thinking about this morning.'

'Of course. I'm sorry, maybe this wasn't a good idea. But we're here now.'

The Warriors' Chapel was a grand, gloomy affair. A high coffered ceiling was hung with ranks of regimental flags, the colours faded and the fabric tattered. Marble-pillared tombs with praying figures and busts of men in periwigs lined the walls. In the middle stood a big box tomb with three effigies lying on it, the tops of their marble heads gleaming in the torchlight like bone.

The chapel was blocked off by a black iron railing. The constable's torch played across the gilt lettering that ran along it: *Veteri Frondescit Honore.*

'How's your Latin?' Sarah asked.

'Rubbish,' said Helen, with a sigh. Ancient something honour? Beneath the Latin motto, the words 'The Buffs: 1572, the Royal East Kent Regiment'. At least they were in the right place.

Helen pushed the gate in the railing. It swung open beneath her hand.

'How often is the chapel used?' she asked.

'Once a day, miss. To turn the pages of the book.'

Helen was about to ask which book he meant when she saw it on a wooden stand to one side of the entrance.

'It's the memorial book for the Buffs,' the man said. 'The record of the fallen. They turn the page at 11am. Not this morning, obviously, what with the cathedral being closed.'

Helen approached the stand. Had William hidden something in the book? But he would have known about the turning of the pages, so he'd know that anything placed in the book would be found the next morning. He hadn't known that the cathedral would be closed that day because of his own murder. And she sensed that the book would be sacred to him, too important to use in a game of hide-and-seek.

Her eyes fell on the heads of the effigies on the tomb beyond the book.

'Can we have a look at these?' she asked. The constable joined her, shone his torch on the marble figures, all lying on their backs with their hands pressed together in prayer. The middle figure was a woman, a coronet on her head, covered to her feet in a long cloak and drapery. Either side of her lay a man in battle dress, armoured gauntlets on their hands and swords by their sides. Each wore an armoured neck-plate and coronet.

'Do you know who these three are?' asked Helen.

'Lady Margaret Holland,' said the constable. 'And her two husbands. She paid for the chapel to be built.'

Helen gazed at Lady Margaret and the two soldiers. She

walked around to the base of the tomb. One man had an alert-looking hound at his feet. Lady Margaret had a pair of puppies. An eagle spread its wings at the feet of her second husband.

No chickens for these brave soldiers. An eagle, though. Helen peered between the eagle's claws, reached in and pulled out the little scroll of rolled-up paper, tied like the others with crimson silk thread.

'Here it is.'

'Well done!' Sarah was as excited as Helen had ever known her. 'What does it say?'

Behind Sarah, in the darkness, Helen saw movement, a figure crouched low, moving across the chapel.

'Watch out!' she called.

The policewoman swung around and gave chase, the constable close behind her. They wasted no breath on shouting. The patter of running feet soon came to an end, and Helen heard a high-pitched yell of protest.

Minutes later, Sarah brought her captive back, wriggling to get away from her hold on his collar.

'Right, then. What are you up to?'

The constable shone the torch at their captive. With a shock, Helen recognised the boy, his eyes wide with panic. He threw up a hand against the light.

'Let me go! I didn't see anything,' he protested. 'I won't tell anyone what you're doing. Promise.'

'Wait,' she said. 'Sarah, I know this boy. Josh, what are you doing here?'

He stopped struggling. 'You?' He pulled his collar away from Sarah Greenley and swung his gaze from her to the constable. He looked enormously relieved. 'Are you the police?' he asked. 'I thought…'

'You thought we were Satanists?' asked Helen, light dawning.

'Yeah. I saw lights moving about in the cathedral. My dorm looks out this way. Fin was too scared to come with me. But I reckoned maybe it was a Black Mass or something, and they were going to murder someone else. And the door was unlocked, so I came in to see.'

The constable drew his brows together. 'You should be in bed, not running around the close. I'll have to report you to the choirmaster.'

'Please don't. I was just worried about what might be happening,' Josh said. 'I'll get into real trouble if you do.'

Helen looked at Sarah. 'Josh was very helpful today, when I was looking for one of the other tombs. And I think he's been really brave, coming in here if he thought someone was about to be murdered. Does he need to get into trouble?'

Sarah sighed. 'Listen to me, Josh. It's dangerous, coming in here alone when you think something bad might be going on. If you're worried, you should tell the choirmaster, or talk to the constables. Is that clear?'

He nodded. 'Yeah.'

'All right. Constable, we've found what we were looking for. Let's leave it at that. We'll see this young man back.'

They walked back to the cathedral door and out into the floodlit close. Sarah's phone buzzed. She took a few steps away and took the call.

'Thanks,' whispered Josh.

Helen grinned. 'No problem.'

'What did you find?' he asked.

'Tell you later.' Helen didn't want to open the paper with the constable and the boy around. The fewer people who knew about William's trail, the better.

130

Sarah re-joined them, a frown on her face. Helen felt a sudden clutch of cold fear.

'Not Greg?' she asked.

The woman shook her head. 'No. Still nothing from the hospital. But that was one of my PCs. She's been interviewing the hotel staff. Can you think of any reason why the man who went to Gregory Hall's room would have dripped water through the lobby?'

'How do you mean?' Helen asked.

'The housekeeper says he walked straight across the lobby, which had just been mopped. She said his shoes and the bottom of his trousers were wet. He left a trail of dirty water across the nice clean floor. She had to call back one of the cleaning staff to clear it up.'

'How strange.' Helen's thoughts went again to the river. God. Had the man been disposing of a body?

'When are the police divers coming?' she asked.

'Tomorrow, supposedly. I see what you're getting at. We'll take another look at the river. Firstly, let's see Josh back to the Choir House. You can lock up behind us, constable.'

The man nodded agreement, although he still looked disapproving.

'I'll be watching you,' he told the schoolboy. Josh smiled his angelic smile. Helen noticed he had pyjamas on under his anorak. She'd never really been interested in children, but she was getting to like this one.

CHAPTER TWENTY-THREE

J osh needed to get rid of his police escort before she and Helen blew his cover. If the policewoman knocked on the door of Choir House, he'd be in deep trouble. All the choirboys had been told under pain of expulsion not to leave the building, after the news came through about the actor getting knifed. The other boys had teased Josh and his two friends, telling them anyone linked to the play was going to die. They were all scared, although they were trying not to show it.

He'd gone out through the back door by the kitchen, evading the kitchen staff who were gossiping loudly about the stabbing. Fin had created a diversion by going in to beg extra flapjack for the dorm, saying the boys were still hungry after supper. He'd refused to come with Josh, partly because he was too scared of what might be happening in the crypt, and partly because of his warning from the choirmaster after Evensong.

'No way, man. I can't risk it,' he'd said. But he'd promised to sneak down and unlock the back door when Josh texted him.

'I just have to make a quick call,' he told Helen and the policewoman. 'I'll catch you up later.'

The policewoman sighed. 'I wasn't born yesterday,' she said. He knew that; she must be about the age of his grandma. He wished she'd go away. He thought he could probably explain his problem to Helen, but police never listened to you. Guilty until proven innocent, his brother said.

'All right,' he said. 'Just let me send this text, then.' He tapped out a quick plea to Fin. 'There. I'll go in the back way, so I don't wake anybody up.'

'You'll come with me,' said the woman. Reluctantly, he followed. As they reached the front door, it opened. He grinned. He was in luck.

'Hello, young Josh.' It was Trey. 'What are you doing out of doors?'

'Thank you,' Josh said, waving goodbye to Helen and the policewoman. He darted in and shut the door. 'I've been helping the police with their inquiries,' he told Trey. 'What about you?'

'Extra patrols,' said the man. 'I was just checking on everything. Making sure there are no windows or doors left unlocked. Like the back door by the kitchen, for example.' He looked stern. 'You shouldn't be out tonight, Josh. Dangerous times. Up to bed and stay there, hear me?'

'Of course.' Josh pulled off his trainers and crossed the hall. He collided with Fin on his way down to unlock the door. Together, they ran back up the slippery wooden stairs. Reaching the first floor landing, they fled down the corridor and flung themselves into the dorm.

It was almost empty; most of the boys went home on Friday night until Saturday Evensong. Of Josh's year group, only the three of them involved in the play remained.

'What happened? We thought you'd been caught and sacrificed.' Ben was sitting up in bed, PlayStation discarded beside him. Both the other boys were in striped towelling dressing gowns and wore posh button-through pyjamas. Josh pulled off his anorak and climbed under the duvet, eager to cover up his cartoon character pyjamas. He was way too old for them now and they were too short around the ankles. Maybe he'd get some new ones at Christmas. Still, Fin and Ben had been too scared to go and explore the cathedral in the dark, and he hadn't.

'They were in the Warriors' Chapel,' he said, settling down. 'They'd gone right inside, where the statues are having a threesome.' The boys giggled. They all thought that tomb was funny, the woman in the middle and the men lying on either side. 'They found something,' Josh said. 'Something in the tomb. I don't know what. I was trying to get close enough to see, and they saw me.'

'Oh my God!' Fin's eyes were wide. 'They could have killed you.'

'I legged it. But they chased after me, and caught me,' he continued. 'I was pretty scared.'

'What did you do?' Ben always tried to sound laid back, but Josh could see he was as excited as Finlay.

'Turns out it wasn't Satanists, though,' Josh said. 'It was the police. Investigating the murder, for clues.' He stretched out and smiled. 'I helped them a bit, then decided I might as well come back. I was about to shake them off and come in the back way, when Trey opened the front door.'

Fin was shaking his head. 'You got lucky, man. What if it had been someone else?'

Josh was overtaken by a huge yawn that almost dislocated his jaw. 'I'd have thought of something.' He felt invincible, forgetting how scared he'd been in the cathedral when the police chased after him. He was a hero.

Something nagged at his memory. Something to do with the river. But he was tired. It had been a long day. He yawned again.

'Here. We saved you a bit.' Finlay shoved a lump of flapjack at Josh. He unwrapped it from the paper napkin, which stuck to it in places, and started to eat.

Something about the river.

Chewing, he reached out and put out his bedside light. He'd clean his teeth in the morning.

#

Josh was rocking smoothly from side to side, listening to a gentle sound: plash, plash, plash. His hand trailed in the water, which was running cool and clear. Strands of weed caught in his fingers. Then something else – something slimy and horrible. He pulled his hand out of the water, saw it red with blood.

Someone called his name. 'Josh! Where are you?' His mother, her voice anxious. He had to get back, had to go on stage. He'd miss his cue and be thrown out of the choir. He tried to sit up and found he was unable to move, pinned down in the bottom of the boat by a blanket tied tightly around his chest.

With an enormous effort, he yelled for help. 'I'm here,' he called, throwing off the blanket and sitting up.

'Shut up, Josh,' murmured Fin, sleepily. Something – one of Ben's socks, by the smell of it – landed on his head.

Shit. He flopped back down in bed, heart thumping. A nightmare. He grabbed at the shreds of it as they disappeared through his fingers: the weeds in the river; the blood on his hands. The plash, plash, plash of the boat being rowed through the water.

Wait. He opened his eyes wide in the darkness. There had been a real boat, going down the river in the dark. The night of his performance, when he stood outside the theatre in the drizzle. The night the old man was murdered in the cathedral.

Josh had walked along the river path, then turned and seen the canoe pass by him, heading under the bridge. He tried to remember more. He hadn't seen the face of the canoeist. But he had the impression of a big man with strong shoulders.

He'd thought at the time it was strange, going rowing in the dark and the rain. What had the policewoman said? Can you think of any reason why the man who knifed the actor would have wet feet? Well, he might if he'd been paddling a canoe. The boys had been taken canoeing in the summer from a water-sports centre just outside Canterbury. It had been brilliant and they'd all got soaked. Josh remembered the instructor, standing knee-deep in the water as he'd steadied the canoes for them to get in.

'Fin?'

'I'm asleep.'

'Listen. I know something about the murderer.'

A sigh, and Josh heard the boy roll over. 'Go on, then.'

'He's got a canoe. He went right past me, on Thursday night, outside the theatre. But it was dark, so I don't think he noticed me.'

Fin yawned. 'How do you know it was him?'

'Because the police said he had wet feet.' Josh explained what he'd heard from the policewoman and Helen. 'The man who stabbed Gregory Hall had been in the river. The police are going to get divers to search it. I think we should go and look for the canoe.'

'It doesn't mean it was the man you saw,' objected Fin. 'That would never stand up in court.' Finlay's father was a barrister and he considered himself an expert on legal matters.

'Maybe not, but we should have a look,' Josh said. 'The canoe was going under the bridge by the theatre. So it must have come past the park where the Beerling Hall is, then... where does the river go, after the bridge by the theatre?'

'Dunno.' Finlay sat up and Josh saw the blue light of his phone. 'Let's look on the map.'

Josh hopped out of bed and sat next to him. Fin's phone had a much bigger screen than Josh's embarrassingly old one, which used to be his sister's. Fin's dad always got him the newest iPhone as soon as it came out.

'It goes right through the middle of town,' Fin said, zooming in on the map. 'Look. That's the High Street. And that's where they do the boat tours from, down that alley. Do you remember? Are you sure it wasn't one of those boats?'

'Yeah. Like they'd be doing that in the rain? Anyway, it was just one bloke.' Josh and the other boys rather admired the students who did the tours, skilfully punting the wide flat-bottomed boats full of enormous American tourists along the narrow twists and turns of the river. They'd taken the tour themselves once when Ben's father had treated them all.

'Eastbridge Hospital,' Finlay read. 'It goes right underneath. I don't remember there being a hospital.'

'It's not a real one,' said Josh. 'It's one of those pilgrim places, like Beerling Hall.' Eastbridge. Helen had been looking for something to do with Eastbridge, in the cathedral. The tomb of the master of Eastbridge, where she'd found the bit of paper. Was that where the man was going?

He followed the river along. 'Greyfriars Gardens. Is that where the island is?'

137

'Yeah. Then it goes under the main road. Maybe he was escaping and had a getaway car down there,' said Fin. 'If it really was the murderer.'

'Do you think we could get a canoe?' asked Josh. 'Like, from that place where we went in the summer? We could go all the way along the river, look for clues.'

'Maybe.' Finlay yawned. 'Let's talk about it in the morning. I'm knackered.'

Josh couldn't get back to sleep. He lay awake, listening to the boys' snuffling and snoring, thinking about the river.

CHAPTER TWENTY-FOUR

By mutual agreement, Helen and Sarah headed for the nearest pub. It was a traditional Tudor hostelry, decorated with horse brasses and dried hops. The low ceilings and small round tables made Helen feel like a giant. She ducked under the beam in the doorway between the bar and the snug, managing not to bump her head as she balanced two glasses of wine through the throng of Friday night drinkers.

'Let's have a look at it, then.'

Helen unrolled the small scroll of paper. The writing, like the others, was neat black ballpoint.

'I suppose we should check whether this is actually William's handwriting,' she said. 'I wonder who would know.' The warden, maybe. Canon Bryce, perhaps – but she wasn't sure if the man was trustworthy. Alice would know. She thought again of the elderly woman, out there somewhere in the dark.

Helen read aloud, 'Remember the number of the steps.'

'What steps?' asked Sarah.

Helen thought. 'Not sure. The pilgrim steps, maybe? I walked up them today, from the choir to the Trinity chapel, where Becket's shrine used to be. They're shallow, worn away in the middle. They've been there since the Middle Ages.'

'I don't suppose you counted them?'

'Nope.' Helen tried to remember how long it had taken her to walk up, the rhythm of the climb, to get some idea of how many. Twenty, perhaps? Thirty? 'I suppose we could go back,' she said, without enthusiasm.

Sarah yawned. 'Not tonight. I need to grab an hour or two of sleep, then I'm heading back to the office. I've got one murder, one attempted murder and a missing person inquiry to co-ordinate. All since you came to town, Helen. You do seem to bring trouble with you.'

All since the premiere of the play, Helen thought. Which, of course, she had brought with her. She took a sip of wine, tried to forget about Charlie's talk of curses.

'I'm sorry,' she said. She thought again of the river by the theatre; the man with the wet feet. The idea of Alice's body lying undiscovered among the weeds haunted her. 'How can you not have found her yet?' she burst out.

Sarah put her glass down and gave Helen a level look. 'We have twenty officers searching for her. We've pinpointed where she was last seen. We've done house to house, plus one search of the river, and we'll send the divers in tomorrow. Unless there's something else you can tell me, I don't know what more I can do.'

Helen was silent.

'Well? Is there something?' Sarah regarded Helen wearily.

Helen shook her head. 'I mean… you already know it's probably something to do with Thomas Becket. And the play, which supposedly gives away his burial place.'

'And does it?'

Helen nodded. It didn't seem to matter now about keeping the secret. Not with Greg clinging to life in hospital and Alice

140

still missing.

'Yeah. It's in the epilogue, which has not been published or performed. William had hidden it in the library. I talked to the librarian, Canon Derek Bryce. Remember? He was the one who discovered William's body with me.'

Sarah leaned forward, pressed her fingertips together. 'Tall man, thin and surprisingly composed for someone who'd just found a near-decapitated body.'

'That's him. Anyway, he says the epilogue has gone missing. That's what we're looking for with this paper-chase around the tombs.' She paused. 'He was being a bit odd about it. But I haven't seen him since this afternoon. He doesn't know about this last clue. The Buffs.'

'Odd how?'

Helen described his behaviour in the Deans' Chapel. 'I don't know. It's like he was really stressed about something.'

'I know how he feels,' said Sarah. 'OK, I think we should talk to him again. He should have told us about the missing epilogue, for a start. As should you.' She stood. 'I'm off. Maybe I'll call on him tonight. It's always nice to catch them unprepared.'

Both their phones rang, simultaneously. Helen grabbed hers from the sticky table, checked the number. It was Henry Gordon, the theatre director. Quickly, she answered, heart hammering.

'Helen? Greg's awake. Looks like he's going to make it.'

'Thank God.' Helen found herself on the verge of tears, her throat catching as she laughed in relief. 'Thank you. Thank you so much.'

She glanced across at the policewoman, whose stern face had broken into a smile.

'Good news,' she was saying into her phone. 'OK, I'll be over there as soon as I can.'

They faced each other, Helen wondering how pissed off with her Sarah really was.

'No rest for the righteous,' said Sarah, holding out her hand. 'I'm off to the hospital.' Helen was forgiven. They shook hands a little awkwardly and the policewoman left.

Helen sipped her wine. The police would be focused on Gregory Hall and his attacker, now the actor had come round. So who would be out there, looking for Alice in the river?

She couldn't go back to her hotel and sleep, knowing Alice was still missing. She rummaged in her rucksack. The head torch she'd bought the previous year was tucked away in one pocket. She pulled a fold-up waterproof jacket from her bag and put it on. It was thin, but the night was not cold. Her walking boots were sturdy. She was as ready as she'd ever be.

Helen left the pub and walked through the dark, narrow streets to where the river ran past the theatre. The street was deserted. Helen leaned against the parapet of the bridge, fixed the torch on her head and switched it on. The vibrant green weeds streamed away in the current. The river was shallow – no more than knee-hight, she guessed – but fast-flowing. She'd need to be careful.

First, she walked downstream, along the riverside path that ran along the bank next to the theatre's modernist bulk. The sculpture of a huge metal face loomed out of the darkness as her torch caught it, its brooding expression taking on a new menace. For a moment, she thought the man on the bench was real, and started to apologise for shining her torch on him. Another sculpture, she realised. She was twitchy, half-expecting the statues to speak, to warn her off.

She turned back to the river, paying attention to the under-growth on the bank. She probed with her torch, both hoping and hoping not to find something. What was she looking for? Clothing, perhaps. Not just clothes. She was looking for Alice's body, but she couldn't admit that possibility, even as she searched.

She quickly ran out of riverside path. The path skirted around an old brick building, which looked like it dated back many centuries. Beyond it, Helen stood at the locked gate of a park. 'Abbots Mill Gardens: closed at dusk,' she read. She peered through, seeing a smooth sweep of lawn running down to the river. It looked like a well-used path; unlikely, perhaps, that anything would go unnoticed on that stretch.

She turned back, walked upstream to the theatre. On the far side of the bridge, buildings backed onto the river, their foundations disappearing into the water. If she wanted to explore in that direction, she thought, she would need to do it from the river itself. And she'd have to go under the bridge to get there.

Carefully, she shuffled down the steep bank, muddy from the recent rain. Her foot slipped on the greasy clay and plunged, knee-deep, into the water. Damn, that was cold. She steadied herself and lowered her other foot into the icy stream.

The bridge was low. She felt a return of the claustrophobia that haunted her in enclosed spaces. But the river was shallow, reaching only mid-way up her shins. If she bent over, she'd have plenty of space to get through. The bridge wasn't that wide; just the width of the two-lane road that crossed it.

She reached her hand up to the flint of the bridge wall, bent her head and shone the light down the tunnel. The walls were smooth, the old bridge having been reinforced with concrete at

143

some point. Damp marked the surface, sweating into patches of green mould.

The water pushed hard against her legs, splashing above her knees. She swallowed down her fear and walked into the tunnel.

She inched forward, feeling her way with her feet, her hands skimming moss and lichen. She couldn't lift her head to see how far she had to go; had to keep her eyes and torch fixed on the pebbles beneath her feet. She hit a stone and stumbled, clutched in panic at the arch, managed to keep her footing. Maybe this hadn't been such a good idea.

She searched the river bed, sweeping the torch from side to side, scanning for – whatever she was looking for. Sarah had said the man who'd stabbed Greg had wet feet. If he'd been in the river, could he have dropped the knife there on his way back? Helen should keep her eyes open for knives, too.

The sky opened up above her head. She'd made it out the other side of the bridge. Straightening, relieved to stand tall again, she waded up the river, past old buildings of red brick, their crooked walls meeting the water. Clumps of vegetation – buddleia and brambles – grew out of the crumbling masonry. Weed wrapped around Helen's legs, slowing her progress. She walked next to the wall, one hand out to steady her in the fast current. Her feet were numb with cold.

In any other circumstances, she would have relished the chance to see the old city from this unexpected perspective. Houses cantilevered out over the river, black oak beams holding up whitewashed walls and cross-leaded windows.

She came to a platform with a raft of flat-bottomed boats moored alongside, the tourist punts that she'd noticed earlier in the day. She swung the torch beam into the bottoms of the boats, pushed them apart to probe the water underneath. They clunked gently together.

Beyond the platform, another bridge loomed, this one with two arches: one small and one wider. These tunnels went under Canterbury High Street, Helen realised. And on the other side of the bridge, Eastbridge Hospital itself.

Helen paused alongside a black-and-white Tudor building, a popular restaurant with customers still visible in the lit-up windows. She kept back into the shadows at the side of the river, her torch beam focused low on the water. She didn't want to be asked what she was up to.

This tunnel would be longer, darker. The High Street was wider than the narrow road over the river by the theatre. And then the river disappeared below the Eastbridge buildings. Helen wasn't sure how far she would need to walk, back bent to the water.

She pointed the torch into the bigger of the two tunnels, trying to see to the end. Definitely longer. Was it lower than the other one, too? She couldn't be sure. The arch was brick-built, with vegetation growing out of the cracks. She saw iron hoops built into the sides of the tunnel, chains looped along the length of it. For mooring boats, perhaps? There was something, a bulk of some sort, tethered to the chains further into the tunnel.

God, thought Helen, stomach tightening. What is that?

She took a breath and bent low. Time to find out. She moved more confidently now, feeling her way, less oppressed by the closeness of the arch over her back. She stopped every few paces, trying to make out the bundle. A boat, perhaps. A canoe? She was almost there.

A few steps more, and the ground disappeared beneath her

foot. She gasped as her ankle plunged into a hole, twisting painfully. She flailed for a second, trying to keep her balance, then fell into the dark water.

The current took her, spun her around. Helen tried to reach the river bottom with her hands to push her face back above the surface. But her foot was stuck at the wrong angle and she was no longer sure which way was up. She had water in her mouth, in her nose; felt a desperate need to cough.

As she tried to kick free, she realised what a hopelessly stupid thing she had done. She was alone, at night, trapped under a bridge in the water. And nobody knew where she was.

CHAPTER TWENTY-FIVE

Alice set the Bible aside. It was too dark to read now, and as was so often the case, she found that reading the scriptures brought more questions and doubts than comforting answers. But it was a way to connect herself back to Mark, to the firm faith he had held, which had grown and strengthened throughout their marriage.

She remembered long evenings in the vicarage, the pair of them sitting companionably at the kitchen table, Alice deep in her research and Mark writing his sermon for the week. Occasionally they would both reach at once for the same battered black Bible, one of the many books that piled high on the table. Eventually, one of them would feel hungry and they'd push the books aside while Alice made cheese on toast or heated up some soup. Poor Mark, she thought. At least I fed the children properly.

Not that he had ever complained. He'd known what he was getting when they married. Mark had been a theology lecturer at the School of Oriental and African Studies, almost twenty years older than Alice when she arrived at the London university aged twenty-one. At the time, Alice had been interested only in studying Islam as a way to better understand the countries of north Africa and the Middle East, where she had spent much of her childhood with her diplomat parents.

It was Mark who had opened Alice's eyes to the similarities between the three Abrahamic faiths. Their research interests had converged as their romance bloomed, and they had spent the early years of their marriage travelling and working in the Middle East. She would happily have settled in Jordan, where they were living when Mark announced he wanted to train for the ministry. By then, she was pregnant with the first of their boys, and it seemed sensible to go back for the birth. They'd swapped sunshine and oranges, not to mention the ancient mysteries of the Holy Land, for the drab drizzle of 1970s England. Everyone had told her how happy she must be to be home.

Alice sighed. Reminiscing was getting her nowhere. It was too dark to read, too cold and uncomfortable to sleep. And if Jean was right, this was her last night on earth. She didn't want to waste it.

Tell me what to do, Mark, she implored him. You always seemed to know what to do.

Mark had been the one to take charge when Jean had tried to blackmail poor Derek Bryce.

Alice had been appalled when Derek had confessed to them his affair with Jean, judging him for his taste as much as his lapse in morals. She had wondered for months why their intelligent young curate had been backing Jean in her attempts to gain power on the Parochial Church Council, speaking up in her favour when Jean sought to exclude women she saw as unsuitable from the flower rota or the Mothers' Union. Derek had been studious, interested in Alice's research, curious about other religious traditions. She had been unable to understand his infatuation with the small-minded woman and her petty quarrels.

Mark, more worldly than her at times, had understood. 'She's incredibly sexy,' he'd explained gently to his wife. 'Some men like that ice-maiden image. Sorry, that's just the way it is.' He'd laughed at her horrified face. 'Not me, obviously. Promise.' But she'd noted the twinkle in his eye.

Jean had expected Derek to marry her. She'd announced their engagement at the Parochial Church Council, to the horror of everyone, including Derek. 'Once my divorce has come through, obviously.' Alice had watched the colour drain from Derek's face.

'We have to save him,' she'd told Mark. 'It'll ruin his life.'

Jean's spite, when Mark made her realise Derek was not going to marry her, had almost ruined him anyway. She'd told Mark – and her husband, Tim – that Derek had been abusing her son. She had offered no proof, and Oliver had refused to say anything when Mark had gently questioned him about it.

Mark had taken the brave – and at the time unusual – step of calling the police. They'd investigated, and found no evidence. Eventually, Jean had tearfully admitted she'd made it up to get her revenge on Derek. Shortly afterwards, the family had moved away. Alice heard on the parish grapevine that Jean and Tim had soon divorced.

Derek, saved from a marriage which filled him with horror, had retreated into his studies. He had remained friendly with Mark and Alice, although he had been so traumatised by the affair that he sought a posting in the north of England and worked in Durham for many decades. Only recently had he returned south, when his much-admired work on the history of Durham Cathedral had recommended him for the librarian role at Canterbury. Alice had been pleased to see him back.

They'd discussed with enthusiasm his current project, a life of Saint Augustine, founder of Christianity in Kent.

But now, she wondered uneasily what Jean's re-emergence had to do with Derek Bryce. She thought of Mark's bravery all those years ago.

'There's no point hiding from it,' he'd said. 'You have to confront bullies head-on. You can't bargain with them. Bring their secrets out into the light. Then they have no currency.'

But what if the secrets are not yours to bring out? thought Alice. You kept the secrets of Eastbridge, Mark. Should I not do so too?

CHAPTER TWENTY-SIX

Something had hold of her. It was pulling, dragging her away from the hole where her foot was stuck. Released, Helen broke the surface of the water, choking and gasping in the darkness. She began to flounder, then opened her eyes to the night sky. She'd floated free of the tunnel, brought out of it by the current.

She needed to get out of the water. She pulled on whatever had grabbed her, hauled herself upright and found her feet, standing bent over with her hands on her knees. She coughed, gasped and coughed some more. Her chest contracted painfully, and she spat mouthfuls of water into the river.

'Are you all right?'

She rubbed weed from her eyes and turned to see who had rescued her. His eyes were deep with concern. Helen tried to smile and retched again, bringing up more river water.

'Josh.' Her shoulders heaved as she struggled to regain her breath. 'How on earth...?'

'Come on.' He tugged at her arm, leading her back to where the boats were moored. They heaved themselves up onto the wooden platform. Helen knelt on hands and knees, coughed up more water, spat out weed.

'Feeling better?' asked the boy, politely.

'Yeah.' She sat down, wiped her face with shaking hands. 'Blimey, Josh. I thought I was dead. How did you know... how did you find me?'

He shrugged. 'You'll probably think I'm mad.'

Helen smiled. 'I won't. You saved my life.'

'I dreamed about a boat. That I was lying in the boat, and someone was calling my name. Then I woke up, and remembered the boat I saw before, and that thing the policewoman said about the man with wet feet. I couldn't get back to sleep. I came down here to see if I could find the boat. I saw you going under the bridge, so I followed you.'

'You saw a boat? When?' Helen hugged her knees, conscious that she was freezing cold. The boy was wet through, too; she should get them both somewhere warm and dry.

'During the play, on Thursday night. I went out halfway through and there was a canoe going under the bridge by the theatre. Coming this way. And a big man was paddling it, in the rain.'

A canoe. Helen thought of the shape she'd seen in the tunnel, before she'd lost her footing. Could it have been a canoe, tied up where the chains hung from the arch?

She thought about going back to look, and shuddered. She wasn't sure she could force herself back into the dark waters under the bridge again. And she certainly wasn't going to expose Josh to such danger. She thought again of the way she'd come. It would be a long walk, retracing her steps along the river. And there was the bridge by the theatre to get through. Unless there was another way.

'How did you get here, Josh?'

He pointed behind them. 'There's an alley down to the

152

landing stage, for the boats. We did a boat trip once, Fin and Ben and me.'

Thank goodness. 'OK. We'd better get you back.' She picked up a towel that had been discarded in the bottom of one of the punts. A bit grubby, but better than nothing. She rubbed her face and short hair dry. With a glance at Josh, she turned her back, pulled off her sweater and wrung it out before putting it back on.

'Here. Let me dry you off a bit.' He submitted patiently while she wrapped him in the towel, feeling awkward at the maternal gesture. 'Don't want you to get cold.'

'I can do it,' he said, taking the towel from her. His anorak was mostly dry, just wet around the arms where he'd pulled her from the river. His tracksuit bottoms and trainers were soaked, though. She hoped he wouldn't get into too much trouble.

'I think we should look for the boat, before we go back. I've only just got here,' he said.

Helen shook her head. 'No way. There's nothing down towards the theatre, and I'm not going through that tunnel again. And you shouldn't, either. It's much too dangerous.'

'I thought we could take a boat,' said Josh, looking wistful. 'But they're all chained up.'

Thank goodness for that, thought Helen. She really wasn't up for a late-night trip on a stolen punt with a runaway choirboy.

'We could go round the other way,' he said, scrambling to his feet. 'Come on.'

Helen followed as he jumped from the wooden platform onto the river bank.

'What do you mean?'

Josh was already halfway down a covered alleyway between whitewashed walls.

'It depends if the gates by the Methodist church are open. I suppose we could climb them...' he looked dubiously at Helen.

'I don't think that's a good idea,' she said, firmly.

'But if they are, we can get down to the river on the other side of the bridge.' He ran ahead and lifted the latch of the door at the end of the alley.

Helen followed, emerging into a narrow lane of dark half-timbered buildings. There were no street lights, but at the end of the lane, she could see the bright bustle of the High Street. She squelched after him in her wet jeans and boots, hoping they wouldn't attract too much attention.

She supposed she should insist on taking Josh straight back to Choir House, hand him over to the cathedral constables for safekeeping. But the boy seemed to know where he was going. Helen's own schooldays had instilled in her a horror of being seen as a snitch. She hadn't encouraged him, she thought. If she took him back, as she and Sarah had done only a couple of hours ago, he'd probably just go out again, alone.

He darted down the High Street. Blue railings shut off a gap between the restaurants and shops.

'Looks like it's closed,' she said.

Josh reached in and lifted the latch of the side gate. 'Nope.' He grinned. 'Come on. You can get round the back way.'

He led her round a big chapel building and into the trees. They scrambled through brambles and ducked below low-hanging branches, then skirted a well-kept playing field.

'Where are we?' she whispered.

'St Peter's school. We did a concert with them once. One of the boys showed us this way to the river. We used to go swimming.'

And suddenly, they were again next to the river, which

154

gurgled in the reeds that lined the banks. It was quieter here, flowing more slowly in a wide, shallow channel.

'Look.' Josh pointed downstream. 'That's where we were, the other side of that Eastbridge place.' He turned upstream and pointed again. 'And that's Greyfriars Gardens, where the chapel is. Shall we look along the bank? The boat might be tied up somewhere.'

'OK.' This was such a weird night. Helen forced herself to focus. She was looking for Alice. Alice, or anything Alice might have had with her, or dropped. She walked by the side of the water, trying to see into the reeds. But without her head torch, which had come off in the river, it was hard to see anything. The clouds obscured any light they might have had from the moon or stars. Helen wasn't used to darkness this complete, without street lamps to illuminate and throw shadows.

Maybe she should head back towards Eastbridge, see if that was a canoe moored under the bridge. But, of course, she wouldn't be able to see without her torch. This whole exercise was pointless. She should get back to the hotel, have a hot shower and tell Sarah Greenley about the boat. And she should somehow persuade Josh to go back to bed.

Then she heard it. A gentle splash, paddles dipping in and out of the water. She dropped to her knees beside a clump of brambles. An open canoe was rounding the corner from the direction of Eastbridge.

The man paddling was huge. His broad shoulders powered the canoe through the water. Helen was so close; she could hear his breath coming heavily as he fought against the current. His anorak hood hid his face.

She crouched low, glanced along the bank for Josh, hoping he was out of sight. She couldn't see him in the darkness. The canoe glided past. Cautiously, Helen watched it go. She felt in her pocket for her phone, then remembered. She tried it anyway, but immersion had rendered it useless. As silently as she could, she moved out of the shelter of the brambles and walked slowly along the bank, hoping the man would be too intent on where he was going to glance behind him.

Ahead, she saw Josh scurry through the undergrowth to the water's edge. She caught him up.

'See that?' he hissed.

She nodded, put her finger on her lips.

As they watched, the boat slid below a narrow footbridge.

'It's the same one,' whispered Josh. 'We have to follow him. That's the bridge to Greyfriars' island.'

'Keep well back,' murmured Helen, putting out a hand to restrain him. But the boy was off again.

Greyfriars. Helen racked her memory. The grey friars had been Franciscan monks, big landowners in Canterbury until the Reformation. There was a chapel, something to do with the Eastbridge Foundation. She'd tried to visit before, but hadn't found the path. As Josh said, the chapel was on an island, sitting between two branches of the River Stour. She remembered crossing and re-crossing a pedestrian bridge which had a view of the chapel, walking along rows of houses which all backed onto the river, unable to find her way in.

If the man had been coming and going by canoe – and this was the man Josh had seen on the night of William's murder – and the same man who'd attempted to kill Greg…

Helen began to run.

Alice. Alice might be in the Greyfriars Chapel, if she was still alive.

Josh was on the pedestrian bridge, hanging over the railing.

CHAPTER TWENTY-SIX

'Look,' he said, pointing. 'He's gone up that little stream.'

Helen followed his pointing finger, but could see little in the dark. 'You've got better eyes than me,' she murmured. 'Listen, Josh. I think I know where he's going. We need to get the police.' She thought with frustration of her drowned phone. 'I don't suppose you have your phone with you?'

He shook his head. 'I thought it would look too obvious if I took it,' he said. 'I put a pillow down the bed and left my phone on the bedside table.'

'OK. Then we need to go and get help,' she said.

'Let's just see where he's going,' said Josh, darting back behind her and down to the river bank.

Helen, scrambling after him, lost sight of him for a moment in the undergrowth.

'Wait for me,' she hissed.

She heard him scream, a high-pitched noise that was abruptly cut off.

'Josh,' she yelled, all thought of keeping quiet gone. She crashed through the brambles to the water's edge.

As she reached it, the canoe shot past her, the man manoeuvring it through the current with something – someone – crushed under one arm.

'Stop,' Helen called frantically. Seconds later, the canoe had disappeared from sight under the footbridge, and was rapidly borne away on the current.

CHAPTER TWENTY-SEVEN

Heart crashing, Helen ran to the footbridge. How far could he get in a canoe, with a small, struggling boy trying to get away? Not far, surely. But she needed to get help, and fast.

She ran across the bridge and into a narrow covered alleyway that should have brought her out to the street. This must have been the path she'd missed before, she realised. In the darkness, she stumbled straight into the door at the end. Damn. She felt around for a handle. She grasped it and turned. Locked. But there must be a way out. She shoved the door, trying to force it open. She yelled, hoping to rouse the inhabitants of whichever house she was under, and beat on the wooden door.

Nothing.

Helen took a deep breath. Back to the High Street. She crossed the bridge again, and this time saw the chapel, its high pointed roof silhouetted against the night sky, the narrow building straddling the stream. It looked like a witch's house in a fairy tale.

Alice. Helen hesitated. If she was in there, would whoever had taken Josh be back to finish her off later? Should she not at least check first? But the boy's frantic scream still sounded in her ears. Sorry, Alice, she thought. I know you'll understand.

Josh first.

She turned and ran back along the bank, stumbling over the uneven ground. At the playing fields, she panicked for a moment, unable to remember which way they'd come. She headed towards buildings, found the Methodist chapel again. She rounded it, saw the high gates and ran thankfully towards them.

The side gate, which Josh had opened just half an hour ago, was now locked. God, could she not catch a break?

She grasped the railings and looked through to the High Street. It was still busy with Friday night revellers.

'Help!' she called. 'I'm locked in. Can you call the police?'

A woman in high heels and a tiny skirt staggered over. 'What are you doing in there, darling?' she slurred.

'Leave it. Some nutter,' said a man who was trying to keep the woman upright.

'Please,' shouted Helen. 'A kid's been abducted. I need the police. Can you call 999?'

The man gave her a wary look and backed away. Helen looked at the railings and remembered Josh's earlier suggestion. Maybe she could climb over them. They were high, with spikes at the top. But she didn't seem to have much choice.

She clambered to the top and prepared to swing her leg over the scary-looking spikes. A group of drinkers had gathered to watch.

'All right, what's going on?' A uniformed police officer with a bright yellow jacket made his way through the crowd.

'Thank goodness. Please, help me. A child's been kidnapped, just a few minutes ago.'

'I think you need to get back down from those railings, miss,' he said.

'That's what I'm doing.' Helen climbed down, trying not to slip on the metal railings in her wet boots.

'Now, what's all this about?' He looked her up and down with distaste. 'You're wet. Have you been swimming?'

'I fell in. Listen, this is serious. A boy's been abducted, down by the river. Just now, a couple of minutes ago.'

He looked at her, doubtful, then waved the crowd away.

'All right, you lot, back off.'

'Please,' begged Helen. 'I'm not drunk, or mad. We were down by the river, looking for something. The boy I was with – he's young, twelve years old – was snatched by a man in a canoe and dragged away. It's linked to the murder in the cathedral. DCI Greenley knows about him. Can you call her?' She was shaking with cold now, the shock and her wet clothing sending chills through her.

'You're sure about this?' Helen noticed the change in his tone when she mentioned the policewoman.

'I was there,' she said, through chattering teeth. 'Please, we have to find him. Quickly.'

She gave the man Josh's description and he called it through on the police radio, requesting back-up.

'Which way were they going?'

'Downstream. They'd go under the High Street, right here, then along and out where the theatre is. I don't know what happens downstream of there – I think the river goes through a park?'

'All right. We'll get him. Now, I'd better take your details, miss.'

Helen let out a gasp of relief, which came close to a sob. 'Thank you.'

A police car drew up and a uniformed policewoman got out

160

'What's happening with this missing kid?'

The policeman briefed her. The woman noticed Helen shivering and pulled a foil blanket from the car.

'Here, put that on. Jump in the back,' she said.

Helen jumped, glad of the warmth of the car, and wrapped the foil around herself. They drove the couple of hundred yards to the river path by the theatre.

'Right, Helen. Tell us again what we're looking for.'

'A big man, wearing a coat with a hood. A canoe. And Joshua Jones, a twelve-year-old boy.'

The officers walked along the river path, shining powerful torches into the water and along the banks. One ran ahead, called back from the gate.

'It goes through Abbots Mill Park, but the gate's locked. Is there another way in?'

'Back in the car,' shouted the policewoman. 'Down Blackfriars Street, then Mill Lane. We can get in opposite the Miller's Arms.'

The car accelerated smoothly, the driver flinging it around corners with ease. Helen held onto her seatbelt and listened to the hiss and crackle of the radio as the news of Josh's abduction spread, alerting officers across the city. The radio barked responses, possible sightings and requests for more details.

'How long since it happened, Helen?' called the woman police officer.

'I don't have a watch. But it can't have been more than five minutes before I managed to get out and report it,' she said. She thought with unease of the speed with which the canoe was travelling. How far could it get in five minutes? And how long had it been since?

The car pulled up outside the pub and they all piled out.

Helen ran to the river.

'Look. They can't have got any further by boat,' she called. She pointed to the sluice gates straddling the river, which then disappeared under the wide road junction.

'Right. Helen, back in the car. We'll search the park.' The policewoman stepped over the low railings and ran across a footbridge, the other officers close behind.

A small silver hatchback pulled up alongside Helen. The window slid down and an angry face looked out.

'Helen, what the hell is going on?' DCI Greenwood got out of the car and slammed the door.

'I'm sorry,' Helen said, feeling miserably culpable. 'It's Josh. He must have sneaked out again. I was down by the river...'

'Down *in* the river, by the look of you.'

'Yeah. Anyway, he found me there. We were looking for...' She paused, remembering Alice.

'For what, Helen? For Christ's sake, why can't you just let me and my officers do our jobs? Why do you have to put people in danger?'

'For Alice,' said Helen. 'And I think we might have found her.'

There was a pause. 'What do you mean, you think you might have?'

Helen sighed. 'It would take too long to explain. I think she might be in the Greyfriars Chapel. That's where Josh was grabbed.'

Helen watched the policewoman's brain click through the possibilities as she stood under the streetlamp, a crease between her brows.

'Right,' she said, making up her mind. 'Josh takes priority. We'll get to Alice, I promise, as soon as we have spare bodies. But we know which way Josh was headed. We stay with him.

162

I'm not pulling any of my officers off this until we find him.'

She pulled out her radio. 'All patrols divert to join child abduction search. We're looking for an IC3 male, aged twelve, suspected abducted by an IC1 male, aged about forty, thick-set and six foot tall. Last seen in the vicinity of Greyfriars Gardens, travelling by canoe towards Mill Lane.'

The policewoman came running out of the park. 'We found the canoe, ma'am,' she said, panting. 'Abandoned, just before the lock. No sign of the occupants. But there's a plastic bag in the bottom of the canoe, with a knife. And bundles of clothing. Bloodstained.'

Sarah Greenley nodded once. 'Right. Get SOCOs down to secure it and collect the evidence.' She turned to look across the road. 'What's over there?'

'Woodland on the left-hand side, ma'am. And on the right is the big St Radigund's carpark.'

Sarah rolled her eyes. 'OK. Get someone at the station onto whoever monitors the carpark's CCTV, urgently. The others can start on the woods.' The younger woman ran back to the patrol car.

Sarah turned to Helen. 'We need to focus on finding Josh right now. I have to set up road blocks and search teams. Can I trust you to leave that to us, or do I have to bloody well arrest you to keep you out of trouble?'

'I'll leave it to you,' said Helen, abashed.

'Fine. I'm dropping you at your hotel on my way to the station. I also have to go to Choir House and tell them, and get a family liaison to tell his parents. So my evening is not going to be fun. All I'm asking you to do is to stay at the hotel, and keep safe.'

CHAPTER TWENTY-EIGHT

Helen wrapped herself in a bathrobe and sat on the end of the bed, pleating the pink satin bedspread between her fingers.

She felt awful about Josh. He'd saved her life, and she'd been unable to keep him from danger. She should have insisted he went back to Choir House, seen him home and safe. Now he was at the mercy of a man who had cut two throats in the past two days.

There was a tap on the door. Surprised, Helen opened it a crack.

'I know it's late.' It was Charlie, the assistant director from the theatre. Helen had forgotten she was staying in the same hotel. 'I've been at the hospital. I thought you'd like to know.'

'Come in,' Helen said. 'Tell me about Greg. How is he?'

The woman sat on the bed next to Helen and pulled a half bottle of whisky from her backpack.

'He's doing OK. Fancy some?' She poured shots into the plastic glasses from the bathroom. 'Cheers.'

The spirit warmed its way through Helen's body. She shuddered, realising just how cold she'd been.

'The knife missed the artery. That's why he's not dead,' Charlie said. 'He fought the man off. He's stronger than you'd think, Greg. Works out a lot.' She knocked back the rest of her drink. 'It'll be a while before he's back on stage, of course. The wound needs to heal. He's worried that his voice will be affected, where his throat muscles were injured. That's the worst, for someone like him. He can talk, but it hurts.'

'Did he describe the man?' asked Helen, thinking of the hulking creature who had abducted Josh.

'Big, mainly. Tall, bulky. He was wearing a chauffeur's uniform. Greg hates all that, never uses drivers if he can help it. So he knew there was something weird going on when he opened the door. He's not daft. By the way, he asked about you.'

'Did he?' Helen flushed.

'Yeah. He asked if you'd visit him in hospital. If you were still in Canterbury.'

'Oh. Right, well, of course I will.'

Charlie laughed. 'He likes you, Helen. Question is, how do you feel about him?'

'He seems very nice,' said Helen, stiffly. She felt embarrassed, caught out in a schoolgirl crush on a movie star.

'That wasn't my question,' said Charlie. She put her hand over Helen's. 'I wondered if maybe you preferred girls.'

Helen gently withdrew her hand. 'I'm sorry. That's not me.'

'Ah, well.' Charlie poured another shot of whisky. 'Thought it was worth a try. You give off a bit of a vibe, you know?'

Helen knew. 'Apparently so. Sorry.' It wasn't the first time her androgynous style and cropped hair had led to misconceptions about her sexuality. She didn't care. She felt comfortable with how she looked, and she wasn't looking for a relationship anyway.

She got up and gazed out the window. 'I'm afraid there's

more bad news,' she said. 'Joshua Jones, the choirboy? He's been abducted. The police are looking for him now.'

'What? No!' Charlie dropped the bottle. 'When did this happen?'

Helen tried to explain their nocturnal exploration of the river, feeling anew the stupidity of her actions.

'They think it's the same man,' she said. 'He looked the same sort of build, and the canoe would explain why the man who attacked Greg had wet feet.'

'God.' Charlie stared at the ceiling. 'Weird. You've just reminded me of something.' She shook her head. 'Doesn't matter.'

Helen glanced at the clock and clicked on the TV. 'Sarah said earlier there was going to be a press conference tonight. Let's see if it's on the news.'

The hunt for the man who'd attacked Gregory Hall was the headline item on the news channel. A good-looking policeman blinked in the flickering of a hundred flashlights as the world's media clamoured questions.

'Mr Hall is in a serious but stable condition,' he said. 'We want to interview a male, aged around forty years, with a heavy build.' The screen flashed up a black and white photograph of a man wearing a chauffeur's cap, his face hidden by the peak Charlie leaned forward, peering closely at the screen.

'The man may be dangerous, and should not be approached by the public. He has a tattoo on the back of his hand,' the inspector continued. The camera zoomed in on a scrawl of crudely inked letters, just legible on the man's fist as he leaned on the reception desk.

'Oh shit,' said Charlie. 'Oh, bugger.' She was on her feet, hands pressed to her mouth. She turned to Helen, eyes suddenly hard.

'Right. Get dressed,' she said. 'Let's go to Greyfriars and find Alice.'

'I can't! I promised the police I'd stay here. I haven't got any dry clothes, anyway.'

'I'll lend you some of mine,' said Charlie. 'They'll be a bit small for you. But luckily, I go for baggy styles.'

'We should leave it to the police,' said Helen, uncertain.

'Not if this man is who I think it is,' said Charlie.

'Who?'

Charlie shook her head. 'Tell you later. Come on. I'll get you a sweatshirt.' Helen sighed and pulled on her fake-blood-spattered black trousers from the night before.

Ten minutes later, they were out on the street again. 'Wait,' said Helen. 'How do we get back to the chapel? The gate by the Methodist church is locked. We can't climb over the railings again – there'll be police everywhere.'

Charlie grinned. 'We've got a couple of actors staying in the Greyfriars Tavern on Stour Street.' She fished a set of keys from her pocket. 'You can get to the island by a footbridge through the side door. They showed me when we first arrived.'

The women ran through the dark streets, almost empty of pedestrians now. Charlie was quick on her feet, but Helen's legs were longer and she kept up easily. Charlie still hadn't explained her sudden determination to go to Greyfriars.

'Later,' she'd told Helen. 'Let's get there, first.'

The Greyfriars Tavern was on a quiet side street, a three-storeyed building with the top floors overhanging the street. The windows were dark and the door shut.

'Here.' Charlie unlocked a wooden door to the side of the building, pushed it open and stepped through into the darkness.

Helen followed. The wooden door, she realised, was the one she'd run into earlier that evening in her panic, trying to get help for Josh. The passageway led back to the footbridge over the river. She saw a flicker of light ahead. Charlie was lighting their way with her phone. She caught her up on the bridge.

A half-moon emerged from behind the clouds, casting a silvery gleam over the river. They looked out across the island.

'There. That's it.' Helen pointed left towards the narrow chapel building, its high pitched roof sharp against the sky between two trees.

'OK. Better keep it down. He might have come back.' Charlie's voice was low.

They stepped down from the bridge into long grass, silently walking towards the chapel building, pushing through the vegetation on the uneven ground. Soon, they were standing beside the chapel door, looking up at the dark building.

Helen shivered. Was Alice really in there? And if so, was she alone?

Charlie shone her light on a padlock securing the black-painted door. 'Shit.' She moved around the building, looking in at windows.

Helen took a few steps backwards, trying to see if the upstairs windows were also closed. She circled the building, but the windows were all high and tightly shut.

Back at the door, she reached out and tried the padlock. It clicked open.

'Charlie! It's open,' she whispered. The man had barely arrived at the building before Josh yelled, she remembered. Maybe he'd been in the process of unlocking when Josh disturbed him.

The ground floor held nothing of interest: a bare stone room with narrow windows. Quietly, they tiptoed up the narrow wooden stairs. At the top was another door. Helen turned the handle. Locked. Charlie kicked the door, hard. There was a splintering noise and a gasp from within the room.

'Alice?' called Helen. She joined Charlie. Two more hefty boots to the door, and the frame splintered.

Charlie swung her light around a whitewashed chapel, plain and simple. A crucifix hung on the wall next to a painting of the Virgin Mary. At one end stood an altar with a large Bible. And sitting in the corner, huddled into her raincoat, was Alice.

'Thank God!' Helen rushed across to the old woman, knelt in front of her and gently took her by the shoulders. 'Are you all right? I'm so glad to find you.' Alice felt fragile, her bones thin beneath Helen's hands, but her expression of fear faded, and a beam of relief spread across her face.

'Helen? Oh, my goodness. Is that really you?' Tears spilled over from her bright blue eyes. Her white hair was untidy, her face exhausted in the light of Charlie's phone. 'William?' she asked, her voice urgent. 'Do you know what happened to William?'

Helen's throat closed up. 'I'm so sorry, Alice. He's dead.'

Alice dropped her head. 'Yes,' she said. 'I thought so.' Her shoulders sagged.

Charlie crouched down next to them. 'Come on, Mrs Delamare. We'd better get out of here, before Oliver comes back.'

Alice looked up sharply at her voice. She squinted in the bright light, waved the phone away from her face.

'Charlotte? What are you doing here?'

CHAPTER TWENTY-NINE

Between them, Charlie and Helen carried Alice down the stairs and out of the building. She was almost too weak to stand unassisted.

Outside, Alice put her arms around their necks and stumbled along between them, over the rough ground. They kept silent, although Helen was desperate to know how the two women knew each other. Twice, she thought she heard something, stopped and listened hard. But it was animals rustling in the undergrowth, or distant shouts from the Canterbury streets.

Finally, they reached the footbridge.

'You wait here while I check the street outside,' said Charlie. 'We don't want to bump into him.' She slipped silently through the corridor to the street door.

'Are you OK?' Helen asked. 'We'll get you to hospital. As soon as we're safely out of here.'

'Not yet,' said Alice. 'I need to talk to Charlotte.'

'Who is she...?' Helen started to ask, but then Charlie beckoned from the alleyway.

Outside in the street, they stood and stared at each other.

'I'm so sorry, Mrs Delamare. It was him, wasn't it? Ollie?' said Charlie.

'It was. But he was not alone.'

Helen intervened. 'Look, I'm desperate to know what's going on. But we need to get Alice somewhere safe.'

Charlie jangled the bunch of keys in her jacket pocket. 'Like I said, most of the actors have buggered off. Let's use Henry II's hotel room.'

They slipped through the deserted foyer of the Greyfriars Tavern and up to the actor's recently abandoned bedroom. Helen wrapped Alice in the quilt from the bed and put the kettle on. Charlie raided the minibar and poured them each an inch of whisky.

'Right,' said Helen, when they were all sitting down. 'Who's going to explain? Who is Ollie?'

Charlie knocked back her shot. 'Oliver Forbes. He's my brother, worse luck.' She turned to Alice. 'Is my mother involved?'

Alice nodded. 'I'm afraid so.' She turned to Helen. 'I knew Charlotte and her family thirty years ago, when Mark and I had a parish in Chatham. I hadn't seen them since they moved away.' She smiled at Charlie. 'But I recognised you immediately. You haven't changed that much. I've been thinking about you a lot. You and your brother.'

Helen held out her hand. 'Charlie, give me your phone. Josh is still missing. If your brother has him, we need to tell the police.'

Sarah Greenley answered her phone on the third ring. 'Who is this?'

'It's Helen. We've got Alice Delamare. Please don't be angry. She's safe. We know who kidnapped her, and probably Josh, too. His name's Oliver Forbes.'

She waited a beat as Sarah took in the information and decided what she needed to know. Anything else would have to wait.

'Spell his name for me, and any other details you have.'

Charlie took the phone. 'This is Charlotte Forbes. Oliver Forbes is my brother. He's forty-two years old, six foot two inches tall, fair-haired and built like a tank. He has a tattoo on the back of his hand. OF plus CF. Our initials. Last time I saw him, he was living in a bedsit in Margate, but that was eight years ago and I don't have a current address. He has convictions for animal cruelty, drug offences, assault and wounding with intent. You lot probably have a more recent address for him than I do.'

She took a breath and Helen saw she was trying not to cry.

'He's been in and out of prison since he was a kid. You need to talk to my mother, Jean Forbes. She's the one behind all this.'

Charlie wiped away tears, her gesture brusque.

'The last address I have for her is Rochester. Down by the river, Shorts Reach. I think she's still there.'

She handed the phone back to Helen.

'Who was that?' asked Sarah.

'Charlie, from the theatre. She helped me rescue Alice from Greyfriars Chapel.'

'Indeed.' Sarah packed a lot of meaning into a single word. 'Where are you now? Does Mrs Delamare need medical attention?'

Helen explained about the hotel. 'I don't think she's injured but I do think she should be checked over. Should we take her to the hospital?'

'Not unless it's urgent. I think it's safest to stay where you are for now, until we've located Oliver Forbes. I'll send a police surgeon to check her over, and someone to take her statement

CHAPTER TWENTY-NINE

Keep her warm and make sure she gets plenty of liquids.'

'OK.' Helen looked at Alice's face. She'd closed her eyes, looked exhausted and frail. Helen could see bruising now, around her neck.

'And Helen? Well done. But please don't go off anywhere else. We'll get Josh now.'

Helen handed the phone back to Charlie and made them tea, spooning sugar into Alice's cup. She remembered Henry doing the same for her, only last night. It seemed like much longer. She found a couple of shortbread biscuits.

'Here. The police will send someone, Alice. They need to take your statement. Are you hurt? I can see bruising on your neck.'

The woman sighed. 'It's all right. Oliver got angry.' She looked at Charlie. 'I mentioned your name. It seemed to enrage him.'

Charlie pushed the curls away from her face. 'Yeah, it would. He thinks I betrayed them. I went to live with Dad, after the divorce. My mother didn't forgive me, and Ollie believes everything she says.' She sat on the bed next to the old woman. 'I'm so sorry, Mrs Delamare. After all the trouble my family caused back in Chatham.'

'You were a child, Charlotte. It wasn't your fault.' Alice sipped her tea and dunked her shortbread.

Helen pulled up a straight-backed chair from the desk in the corner. 'Charlie – why do you think your brother did this?' she asked. 'What did he have against Alice?' And William, she thought, although she didn't want to bring the poor man's death up again. And Greg, come to that. 'I mean – I thought it was something to do with the play. Thomas Becket.'

Charlie kicked off her shoes and drew her knees up to her

173

chin, wrapping her arms around her legs.

'I don't know,' she said. 'Like I said, I haven't seen him for years. Last time we met, he tried to strangle me.' She gave a twisted smile. 'Families, eh? But whatever it is, my mother will be behind it. He'll do anything for her. She's the only one who can control him.'

'So why would your mother want to kidnap Alice?' Helen asked.

'I can think of a few reasons,' said Alice. 'We did not part on good terms. But that was a long time ago. This is to do with Thomas Becket.'

'The play,' said Charlie, flatly. 'I knew it. I got a horrible letter from her, after she found out I was working on the production. She said I'd regret it, that it was blasphemous. She's always been interested in the church. I don't know why; I think it's the power. She never had much of it herself. Not with my father or with her rotten family. My grandfather was a horrible man.'

Charlie sighed and shook her head, as if trying to dislodge the memories.

'Anyway, she got herself involved in some weird Christian organisation in Rochester, a few years ago.'

'Christianity in Crisis,' said Helen and Alice, together.

'Yeah.' Charlie looked surprised. 'I think that was it. Last time I saw her, she was campaigning against immigration and Islam. Saying we had to protect our Christian identity. A load of crap, but I'm used to it. She was involved with that priest who died. Father Nash. I tried to call her after his death, cos I knew she'd be upset. But she didn't return my calls.'

Helen and Alice exchanged glances. So it went back to Nash after all. Turbulent from beyond the grave.

'When I heard about the protest outside the theatre, I

expected to see her there. Although I didn't think she'd go this far, obviously. I didn't think of Ollie at all, until we saw the tattoo on the news.' She held out her left hand. 'I had mine erased, but you can still just about see it. CF + OF. I did them both, with compasses and an ink cartridge. When we were little. Us against the world.'

Helen stared at the ghostly shadow of the initials, testament to two troubled children finding comfort in each other.

Charlie laughed. 'I got such a beating. Ollie too, for letting me do his.'

Alice took her hand, patted it gently. 'You poor child. I wish I'd known. I should have helped you.'

Charlie looked at their clasped hands for a moment. 'Never mind. That's just the way it was. Actually, when Helen told me about the canoe, it made me think of Ollie... You know, that was the one thing he really loved at Chatham. Going canoeing on the marina. He was good at it, because he was so strong. And it made him happy, because there was so little he was good at.' For a moment, her face brightened at the memory. 'We all went. It was fun. Do you remember?'

Alice smiled. 'I do. Derek Bryce took you.' She finished her tea and put the cup down on the bedside table. There was colour back in her cheeks and her eyes had recovered some of their sparkle. 'Do you know, I think we should talk to Derek.'

'Canon Bryce?' asked Helen. 'From the library? You knew him, Charlie?'

'Yeah.' Charlie's face had fallen again. 'My bloody mother nearly ruined his life. Don't tell me he's back?'

CHAPTER THIRTY

harlie called a taxi over Helen's protests. She'd
promised Sarah they would stay where they were,
but Alice was insistent.

'Derek knows something about this. I saw him, just before I
went into the Chapter House. He was worried and he wanted
to talk, but I was anxious about being late for the theatre.' She
sighed. 'If only I'd been more patient, maybe some of this could
have been avoided.'

It was long past midnight when the taxi drew up in the
Butter Market before the imposing cathedral gatehouse. The
constable who opened the gate was the same man who'd
accompanied Helen and Sarah Greenley into the Warriors
Chapel. He recognised her, and Alice.

'Mrs Delamare! I thought you were missing,' he exclaimed.

She smiled a Buddha smile. 'And now I am found,' she said.
'We need to talk to Canon Bryce. Can you let us through?'

The policeman escorted them across the close. Helen
glanced up at Choir House, wishing with all her heart that
Joshua Jones was safely inside. There was a police officer
standing by the door and lights showed from the ground floor.
Two pale faces pressed against the glass of an upper window
like little ghosts.

Derek Bryce was a night watcher, too. He opened the door wearing a baggy green jersey with holes at the elbows. His jaw was dark with stubble, echoing the grey hollows under his eyes.

'Alice!' His bewildered gaze took in the three women. If he recognised Charlie, he gave no sign of it. 'What happened to you? Are you all right?'

'Can we come in, Derek? We need to talk.'

'Come through. I've got a fire in the study.' He led them to a cosy book-lined room, shaded lamps on low tables augmenting the glow of the firelight. Helen settled Alice in the winged armchair closest to the flames. She took a patchwork throw from the arm of the chair and tucked it around her.

'We've just found Alice,' she explained. 'She needs to keep warm.'

The woman began to cough, pressing her hands over her mouth, thin shoulders shaking.

'Are you all right? Should I call the police?' Canon Bryce handed over an ironed handkerchief.

Alice shook her head. 'I'm fine, and we've spoken to the police. Derek, this is Charlotte Forbes. I'm sure you remember.'

His face darkened with fear and he stepped back from Charlie, as if she might attack him.

'Charlotte and Helen rescued me,' said Alice, firmly. 'I was a prisoner in Greyfriars Chapel. So you can stop looking at her like that. Now, when did you last see Jean Forbes?'

He turned to the well-stocked bookcase and ran his fingers over the leather spines, as if he would find the answer there.

'Oh, God.'

'It's important,' said Helen. 'Joshua Jones is missing. Oliver

177

Forbes took him.' She leaned against the back of Alice's chair. She hadn't been able to protect Josh, but she would protect Alice with her life.

He raised his head. 'Oliver... Oh God. I know Joshua is missing. The police have been all around the close, searching.' He rubbed his eyes, leaving the bags beneath them heavier than before. 'Right, then,' he said, with a heavy sigh. 'It was Thursday evening, just after I saw you, Alice. She was at Evensong, sitting right at the front. I could hardly concentrate on the service She was smiling at me.'

He shuddered.

'But before then... she turned up at the library, about three weeks ago. It was... I was shocked. I hadn't seen her for thirty years. I had hoped never to see her again.' He looked at Charlie 'Sorry. But it was a nightmare.'

'Tell me about it,' said Charlie. She walked to the French windows and looked out into the dark garden.

'She said she was leading some Christian organisation and that they needed my help. I didn't want to get involved.' He turned his face towards Alice, his eyes desperate. 'I never wanted to get involved.'

'I know, Derek,' she said, her voice soothing. 'Tell me what happened.'

'She said she'd been in touch with the Independent Inquiry into Child Sexual Abuse,' he said, misery in his voice. 'She said she was planning to tell them about me. About what she said I did to Oliver, back in the 1980s. She said there were probably other victims.' He leaned his forehead against the row of books gripping the shelf with his long fingers. 'I didn't do anything I promise.'

Charlie sighed and turned back into the room. 'I know. Ollie told me. Our mother said he had to pretend you'd hurt him, and he was upset because he liked you. Because of the canoe trips. Then she was angry with him because he got confused and didn't know what to say to the police.'

Canon Bryce's shoulders slumped. He grabbed the arm of a chair, folded his long body down into the faded upholstery and screwed his eyes shut. When he opened them, they were wet with tears.

'Thank you, Charlotte. That means a lot. When everyone is accusing you of things you know are false, sometimes you feel like you're going mad. You start to wonder if you have terrible memory loss or something.'

He took a breath and pressed on.

'Jean said there had been a cover up, and Mark had put the reputation of the church before her child. She said things were different nowadays and that victims were believed.'

'Mark did no such thing,' said Alice, crisply. 'He went straight to the police, as you well know. And they found no evidence. Jean was lucky they didn't charge her with wasting police time.'

'I know,' said Canon Bryce. 'But she's right, all the same. It would have been dragged up again, and I'd have been named and had to stand down from my position at the cathedral, and people would say no smoke without fire.'

'What did you do?' asked Helen. 'What did she want?'

'Keys,' said the canon, his voice weary. 'She wanted keys, to the cathedral and the gates. I had some copies made. I thought she'd just come and go with her religious group, do whatever they did.'

God, thought Helen. So that's how they'd got in and out, taken Alice from the Water Tower and escaped after William's murder. Jean – or maybe Oliver – had the keys to the cathedral.

'And then she wanted the play,' Canon Bryce continued. 'She said the Marlowe play being staged at the theatre was a fake and that the real manuscript was hidden in the library. I realised she must have meant the epilogue. I talked to poor William Danbury about it.'

'What epilogue?' asked Charlie, her voice sharp. 'Helen, is there an epilogue to the play? Something we don't know about?'

Helen said nothing. She was thinking hard. How had Jean known there was something in the library? Had Derek told her more than he was admitting?

'It's missing,' said Canon Bryce. 'It seems that William had also been approached, or somehow knew of the threat to it. He hid it. Helen found some clues, didn't you? In the cathedral.' He looked at her narrowly. 'Unless, of course, you actually have found it.'

She shook her head. 'Not yet.' She thought of the last clue that she had uncovered with Sarah earlier that evening. Something about the number of the steps, the pilgrim steps. They'd need to go back and look in the cathedral. She tried to remember what she'd done with the paper. Had it been in her pocket when she'd fallen in the river? In which case, it was probably illegible, a sodden lump of paper in her soaking jeans.

Charlie's phone rang. She listened for a minute, then passed it to Helen.

'Where the hell are you?' Sarah Greenley sounded even more angry than usual. 'I've got a police surgeon over at the Greyfriars Tavern and no-one knows anything about you.'

'We're safe. We're at Canon Bryce's house in the cathedral close.' Helen looked at the man, still slumped in the chair. 'I'm sorry. I'll explain later. Any news about Josh?'

'No. Except we've arrested Jean Forbes. She claims to know nothing about her son's activities, or his whereabouts. I need to take Alice's statement to be sure of her involvement. If I come over right now, will you still be there when I arrive? Or will you have gone off on another wild goose chase?'

'We'll be here,' Helen promised. 'And you need to talk to Canon Bryce. He has something to tell you about Jean Forbes.'

She finished the call and moved to stand in front of the door. She didn't entirely trust the canon, even now. She didn't want him doing a runner.

'The police are coming to talk to Alice,' she said. 'I really think you should tell them what you've just told us.'

He looked at her pleadingly. 'But it'll all start up again,' he said.

'You have to tell them, Derek,' said Alice. 'Remember what Mark said. You have to stand up to bullies. Bring their secrets out into the light. It's the only way to take their power away.'

'Amen to that,' said Charlie. 'Mr Bryce, I don't suppose you have any whisky? I don't know about you, but I could really do with a drink.'

CHAPTER THIRTY-ONE

Jean Forbes was at Canterbury police station being questioned, DCI Greenley told them when she arrived. She was still insisting she knew nothing, but records showed she had made several calls that day to a mobile phone registered in Oliver's name.

'It looks like he's still in Canterbury, by the call signal. So we'll find him,' said Sarah, her voice firm. 'Charlotte, you say your brother will do what she says? We may ask her to call him. See if she can get him to see sense and release Joshua Jones.'

Charlie's face twisted into an ugly half-smile. 'Good luck with that,' she said. 'She's never yet used her powers for good.'

Derek Bryce, Charlie and Helen moved to a room at the front of the house, to give Sarah and the police surgeon privacy to interview and examine Alice. Dark velvet curtains were open, framing the view like a theatre set. They left the main light off, allowing the golden floodlights bathing the cathedral to reflect into the room. Charlie and Derek both clutched glasses of whisky; Helen felt she'd had quite enough for one evening. Charlie's capacity for alcohol was beginning to alarm her. But perhaps, with such a nightmare family, she too would have sought solace in booze.

'What happened to you, after you all left Chatham?' asked

Canon Bryce.

'Dad divorced her,' said Charlie. 'He cited her affair, but he'd been shagging his secretary for months, so it was quite convenient for him really. He got to keep the moral high ground and most of the dosh. He bought a flat in Docklands.

'We moved to Ashford, a crappy little house on a new housing estate. I hated it so much. She was even worse without Dad to keep her in line, so I ran away all the time. Dad got used to me turning up on his doorstep. Eventually, he agreed I could stay, although his girlfriend wasn't impressed.' She laughed. 'She didn't stick around long. But there were plenty of others.'

She turned her back to them, looked out at the golden cathedral. Helen could hear the hurt in her voice and moved to stand beside her.

'I hated leaving Ollie alone with Mum. But he was never going to leave.' She turned to Helen. 'It's hard to imagine, but he was quite a sweet kid when he was little. Before he learned to fight back. It's not really his fault, the way he's turned out. I called social services once, because I was so worried about him. But they believed Mum about Ollie being clumsy and falling over a lot. So it just carried on. That's why they say I betrayed them.'

Charlie broke off and blew her nose. Helen put a hand on her arm, felt how hard she was trembling.

'What a nightmare,' she said.

Charlie shrugged and continued her story. Her mother and Oliver had moved around, going from one town to another – Tonbridge, Gravesend, Strood. Oliver did badly at school, dropped out and got involved with small-scale criminal gangs. His brute strength and taste for violence found him a niche as an enforcer.

'She always forgave him. But every time he went to prison, she moved house. Trying to escape his reputation. Then she got this place in Rochester, said it was a step up and she was on her way back.'

'She sounded different,' said Canon Bryce. 'I almost didn't recognise her voice on the phone. But she looked the same.'

Charlie laughed again, her voice on the edge of hysteria. 'Yeah, elocution lessons. She's obsessed with seeming posher than she is. She thinks people look down on her for sounding common. When actually they look down on her for being an evil, manipulative bitch.'

'You did all right, though?' said Helen, gently trying to lead Charlie away from the anger about her mother. 'In the end.'

She nodded. 'Not bad. Yeah. I got to university, studied drama. Then I became an actor. The theatre's full of people looking for a substitute family, so I fitted right in.

'A few years ago, I decided to try directing. Same crowd, but you get a bit more agency.' She grinned. 'I like working with Henry. He's so lazy, I get to make most of the decisions. But he's got the clout to bring in people like Greg Hall, so that's cool.'

She broke off and stared at the cathedral, a golden mass against the dark sky.

'I don't know what will happen now. We really wanted this play to be a success, you know? But after what's happened to Greg... I don't know.'

Canon Bryce got up and joined them at the window. 'Once this has been sorted out... people will want to see the play. It'll be a success, you'll see.' He turned to Helen. 'How far did you get, trying to find the epilogue? Was there anything in the John Boys tomb?'

'Yeah,' admitted Helen. It seemed of little importance now. 'There was another bit of paper, a message in the cushion. It led to the Warriors' Chapel, the Buffs. William's regiment.'

'And what was there?' asked Charlie. 'I really want to know about this epilogue. You should have told us before. Does Henry know?'

Helen shook her head. 'No. Look, it's not even very good, to be honest. The play ends much better without it. But it gives away a secret, and one that should really stay hidden.'

'I thought secrets should be brought out into the light,' said Charlie. 'Rob them of their power and all that.'

Helen sighed. 'I know. To be honest, I would just publish it. But it's not my secret. Talk to Alice about it, later. She'll tell you what she can.'

Helen felt immensely weary. All the effort she'd been to, to find the play and discover the secret. All the blood that had been spilled, the lives lost. If she'd been able to go back, to a branch in the road that allowed her to choose, would she have pursued it?

A memory whispered in her ear. Southwark, the ruins of the old Bishop's Palace. Standing below the tracery of the rose window, Richard listening attentively as she outlined her theory that Christopher Marlowe's last, lost play might have been about Thomas Becket. Richard's excitement, his realisation that this could unlock his research into what happened to Becket's body after the destruction of the shrine.

And he'd asked the question. *Do you want to go on with this? It could be dangerous.* She had been more worried about Richard's feelings for her than the unknown dangers ahead. Full of enthusiasm, falling in love, she'd agreed to work with him. Even with what she knew now, Helen couldn't imagine herself saying no.

'What did you find in the Warriors' Chapel?' asked Canon Bryce, breaking into her reverie. 'I agree with you, Helen. The secret should be kept safe. But if we don't find the epilogue, someone else might.'

She supposed that was true.

'There was another bit of paper. I don't have it with me. I think it might be lost. But it's about steps, something about remembering the number of the steps. I thought it must mean the pilgrim steps in the cathedral. But I don't know how many there are. Do you?'

Canon Bryce reached for his jacket hanging on the back of the door. 'I don't know about you, but I can't imagine sleeping until that boy is found. Let's go and count steps.'

'Beats counting sheep,' said Charlie, yawning. She put down her glass.

Too tired to argue, Helen followed. She cared little now for the epilogue, but like Canon Bryce, she couldn't imagine sleeping until Josh was found. Even if that meant she never slept again.

CHAPTER THIRTY-TWO

Josh's legs shook from the long climb, round and round the narrow spiral staircase. He could see nothing through the thick darkness. The only noises were their footsteps and the man's breathing, right behind him, making the skin scrunch up on the back of his neck.

He started to feel dizzy and his wet trainers slipped on the stone steps. He bumped down painfully on his knees, then slid backwards to land with a thump against the man's legs. The man grunted with surprise.

Josh bit his lip to stop himself crying out with pain and rubbed his bruised shin.

'Get up.'

The man shoved him forward. He scrambled on all fours until the steps widened out to a small platform, a resting place. Cautiously, he felt around, hands flat to the curved brick walls. He found the rough rope handrail that wound around the staircase and hauled himself upright. Then up, still up, inside the guts of the cathedral, feeling his way through its passages in the dark. Behind him, the man breathed heavily through his mouth, huh-huh, like an animal.

When he'd grabbed him back at the river, he'd clamped his big hand over Josh's mouth and nose so tightly, he couldn't breathe, until he stopped screaming for help. He'd tried biting, but the man barely seemed to notice. After the canoe, Josh had been bundled into the boot of a car. That was the worst bit. He always got car sick if he couldn't see out the front and was scared he would choke on exhaust fumes. But it was only for a few minutes, then he was pulled out and carried up the stairs through Queningate and into the cathedral, a hand over his mouth again. The man had marched him across the cathedral to the book stall beside the Warriors' Chapel and unlocked a small wooden door.

That was when Josh had realised where they were going. At the start of term, the older choirboys had been given the chance to go up the Bell Harry tower with a guide. Josh had pretended to be busy with piano practice, even though Fin and Ben knew he hated the piano. He hated heights more, though, and he hadn't wanted them to see that.

He kept climbing, up and up. Hundreds of steps; he lost count after a hundred and ninety. At least while he was climbing, nothing bad happened. He wasn't sure he wanted to get to the top. But finally, the stairs stopped. The space around him widened out and the sound was different. Noises – the scuff of his feet on wooden boards, the huffing breath of the man – echoed. He sensed height above him. The darkness was thinner – light was getting in from somewhere. He stayed low, crouching to the ground. It felt safer there.

The man pushed him out the way and he toppled to one side on the rough wooden floor. He sat and hugged his knees. His tracksuit bottoms were still wet from the river. His legs felt wobbly and his shin hurt. Anyone's legs would shake after that climb. It wasn't because he was scared.

There was a blinding burst of light. Josh squeezed his eyes

closed, then peered through his fingers. A bare bulb hung from a wooden beam, the light dazzling after the darkness.

They were in a big square room, the walls made of dusty red bricks. They must be halfway up the tower, or maybe at the top, Josh thought. The room was mostly empty, apart from a huge wooden wheel in the middle, about twice the height of the man.

Ben had told him about the wheel after the choir tour – like a big hamster wheel, he'd said, a treadmill to pull up stones and stuff when they were building the tower. Holding it upright from the centre was a massive wooden beam, with a rope and pulley system attached. And hanging from the rope was a big iron hook, dark with rust.

It was the hook that did it. All Josh's fears rushed into his chest.

'Please let me go back down,' he said, tears spilling onto his cheeks. 'I swear I won't tell anyone I saw you. I'll never say anything to anyone.' His chest heaved with tight sobs. 'Please. I need to see my mum. She's not well. She'll be worried.'

'Shut it.' The man was cross-legged on the wooden floor, leaning against the bricks and staring at him with dull eyes. His face was pudgy with pale, sweaty flesh. It was the first thing he'd said for ages. Was that good, that he'd started talking?

Josh squashed the sobs back down, tried to breathe smoothly, like the boys were taught in singing lessons. He wrapped his arms around his chest, feeling his heart thump. The man hadn't hurt him, yet. He needed to keep calm. He shoved away all thoughts of his mother.

You're supposed to talk to people who take hostages, Josh knew that from TV. Keep him talking. That's what they always said, muttering it into earpieces as the cops tried to talk some

189

gun-toting villain into coming out with his hands up. He rubbed the tears from his face, tried to think of something to say.

The man was sitting on a bundled-up sleeping bag and pillow. A water bottle and a plastic bag were shoved into the corner behind him.

'Do you live here?' asked Josh, surprised. 'I mean, I won't tell anyone. I just wondered.'

The man shrugged, said nothing.

'It's a cool place to live. But it must be dead loud when the bell rings. It sounds loud from Choir House, and that's not so close. Does it hurt your ears? I like the sound of the other bells more than this one. What about you?'

The man pulled out a mobile phone from his anorak, looked at it and threw it down next to him.

'Have you got any good games on that?' Josh persisted, trying to keep his voice even. 'What do you play?'

'Stop talking!' the man shouted. The phone rang, making them both jump. The man snatched it up, checked the screen then answered, his face set.

'All right, Mum?' His voice was wary. Josh recognised the look on his face: he was expecting a telling-off. The man listened for a moment, eyes on the ground. 'In the cathedral. Up the tower,' he muttered.

He glanced at Josh, then got to his feet and prowled around a square of wooden railings in the centre of the room, underneath the big hook. The wooden floor inside the railing was cut away, showing the bricks beneath. That must be the top side of the fancy ceiling that you could see from inside the cathedral, Josh realised, just before you got to the choir. The area beneath was always full of tourists gazing upward.

CHAPTER THIRTY-TWO

He swallowed, remembering how high up it looked from the ground.

The arched windows around the tower room were mostly blocked out, although one glowed faintly gold. The floodlights, Josh thought, lighting up the cathedral for miles around. He wondered if anyone would be able to see if he waved at the window. Quietly, he stood and edged around the room.

'I'm sorry.' The man's voice was sulky. 'Someone came. I had to leave her.' Josh couldn't hear what his mum was saying to him, but he was obviously getting a right ear-bashing. Josh reached the bright window.

'Sit down!' The man had turned and seen him. Josh froze.

'Yeah, there's... there's something else. There's a kid with me,' he said. 'He was spying on me, at the chapel. So I took him.'

Even at a distance, Josh could hear the squawk of outrage from the phone. He sat, sliding down with his back to the wall. The man turned his head away. He tried to whisper, but there was no mistaking his words.

'What do you want me to do with him?'

Josh held his breath. He heard laughter, a tinkly sort of laugh like girls did when they were showing off. He couldn't make out the words of the woman's reply.

The man took the phone from his ear, stared at it a moment, and then put it in his pocket. He turned to face Josh, his expression uneasy.

'Don't keep moving around,' he said.

'What did she say?' asked Josh. He wasn't sure he wanted to know.

'Nothing. Shut up. Stay still.'

'All right.' Josh glanced again at the tower windows. 'Can I look out of the window, though?' he asked. 'It must be a sick view.'

The man grabbed him around the waist and lifted him off the ground. Josh squeaked as he was shoved up against the window. He could hardly see anything, just the floodlights dazzling through the glass, an impression of the darkness beyond.

'That's... I can't really see,' said Josh. 'Thank you, though.'

The man set him down again. Josh stumbled back a few paces into the wooden rail. He grabbed at it to get his balance, then turned to look down.

In the middle of the exposed brick floor, there was a round wooden section, about a metre and a half wide. It had rope handles looped from both sides. The hook from the pulley dangled right above it.

He knew what that round wooden thing was. When you looked at it from underneath, in the cathedral, it seemed really tiny – a small circle with a blue shield and a white cross. The trapdoor, in the middle of the ceiling, which had been used to bring up the building materials.

'What are we doing up here?' he asked, filled with dread.

The man sat down again and indicated that Josh should do so too.

'Shut it,' he said. 'I'm trying to think.'

Josh sat quietly for what seemed like hours. He could see the man was used to it from the way he sat cross-legged, staring at his hands. His eyes were unfocused, his mouth slack. What was he thinking about?

'I'm Josh,' he said, eventually. 'What's your name?'

The man looked up, his brows lowered. 'None of your business.'

'OK. Sorry. I just wondered. I was thinking about my mum.

I expect the police have told her I'm missing by now. She'll be worried. She'd like to know that I'm safe, with you. Can I call her to explain? I mean, you've already told your mum where you are. I expect she was worried, too.'

To Josh's surprise, the man smiled. It wasn't much of a smile, a secretive lift of the corners of his mouth. He looked down again, his eyes back on his hands.

'No,' he said.

'Bet she was,' Josh said. 'All mums worry, even when you're grown up. That's what mine says, anyway.'

The man glared at him. His smile had gone. 'Shut it,' he said again. He checked his phone and his mouth turned down. He kicked it across the floor, got up and moved to a metal box by the side of the pulley. He pushed a lever, then started to turn a metal wheel, like a car steering wheel, on the side of the box. There was a horrible screeching noise, metal scraping against metal. Above Josh's head, the rope started to run over the pulley. The iron hook moved.

'What are you doing?'

The man didn't answer; didn't even look up. He lowered the hook to just above the wooden circle. He's trying to get it into one of the loops of rope, Josh realised. He lifted and lowered it three times, but it wasn't lined up properly.

'Down,' the man said. Josh looked at him, not understanding. He pointed. 'Get down there.'

'That doesn't look safe,' said Josh. His voice had gone high and squeaky. The man grabbed the back of Josh's neck, squeezed hard. It really hurt. 'OK, OK.' He looked down at the brickwork. It had been there for ages, hadn't it? People must have walked on it before. And he wasn't that heavy.

He scrambled down the wooden structure and onto the

bricks. It was dusty down there, covered in grit and pigeon droppings. The man lowered the horrible iron hook down until it was almost touching the trapdoor.

Josh reached out and grabbed for it. He missed, almost falling down onto the wooden door. Oh, God. This was horrible. He bit his lip hard, tried not to cry. He knelt by the side of the trapdoor, hooked his right arm tightly around the wooden railing. With the other hand, he reached again for the metal hook. It felt scratchy and cold against his fingertips. It moved away as he touched it, then swung back. He seized it. It was heavy, almost pulling him off the bricks and onto the trapdoor itself. He heaved it back, towards the loop of rope. It didn't quite reach.

'Let it down a bit more,' he called. With the extra couple of inches of rope, he could get the tip of the hook under the handle. 'There,' he shouted, relieved. He inched backwards, started to climb up the wooden railings.

'Stay there,' said the man. The great wooden trapdoor started to lift.

Josh wrapped his arms around the railing as the wood creaked and squealed. He felt sure you were supposed to lift it from both handles at once. The wood bowed, then cracked with a shower of splinters. The wooden circle broke in two, one half lifting free while the other stuck in place.

Josh clung tightly to his railing. The man swung the broken half of the door away. A semi-circle of blackness opened up. Josh didn't know how high the tower was. But he knew one thing: falling through that gap would mean instant death.

Gazing into the darkness, almost too scared to breathe, he heard a noise down below. It was a small noise, but Josh's hearing was sharp. A door creaking open. Was someone coming?

He glanced up at the man. He was busy trying to get the broken half of the trapdoor over so he could unhook it. He hadn't heard anything.

Josh lay flat on the bricks and looked through the gap. A pulse of light swung across the darkness of the cathedral. It came back again. He heard a low murmur of voices.

They must be looking for him! Someone knew he was here. Thank God. He took a deep breath, ready to yell for help – then stopped. It would take them ages to get up the stairs. He looked at the man again. He could do anything while they were on their way up. But Josh had to find a way to tell them where he was. And to warn them to keep quiet, so the man wouldn't know.

The man lowered the hook, empty now. It hung over the semi-circle of darkness. Josh swallowed. He really didn't like the hook.

Above him, the wooden railing creaked. The man was climbing down to join him.

CHAPTER THIRTY-THREE

Canon Bryce unlocked the south door near the Warriors' Chapel. 'The pilgrim steps are on the north side,' he said. 'We can cross through the passage under the quire.'

Helen followed him inside, Charlie close behind her. It was pitch dark until Canon Bryce switched on his torch – and even then, the feeble beam of light did not pierce far in the huge vault of the nave. The silence engulfed them.

'Shit,' whispered Charlie. 'It's a bit spooky, isn't it?'

'Just a bit,' Helen said, turning to smile at her.

A pure unearthly note sounded in the silence, high and clear as a bell. A boy's voice soared high into the register.

'*O vis eternitatis…*' The sound echoed around the vast space. Josh. The music he'd sung at the beginning of the play. He was here, somewhere in the cathedral.

'*In silencio perfecto…*' the voice continued, before stopping abruptly with a shriek.

Helen clutched Charlie's arm. Charlie put her fingers to her lips and gestured to Derek Bryce to switch off the torch.

'It's Josh. I chose that music myself: Hildegard of Bingen. But he's changed the words,' she whispered. 'That *in silencio* bit. He's telling us to keep quiet.'

They stood and listened, straining their ears. 'I just wanted to see what the echo sounded like…' The voice came faintly, high above their heads.

Helen lifted her eyes to the vaulted ceiling. Right up in the centre of the tower, a hundred feet or more above their heads, she could see a light. She pointed.

'Bell Harry Tower,' whispered Canon Bryce. 'Looks like the trapdoor is open.' He moved towards the door. 'I'll get the police.'

'Wait,' Helen said. 'How do I get up there?'

'Helen, no. It's too dangerous,' he said.

'Tell me,' she hissed.

The canon hesitated, then pointed towards a small door behind a counter piled with guidebooks. The door stood ajar. He pressed the torch into her hands and slipped out of the cathedral.

Helen pushed through the door and shone the torch upwards. She was at the bottom of what looked like a very long spiral staircase.

'I'll come with you,' said Charlie. 'He's my brother.'

'And Alice said just the mention of your name made him angry. I'll go alone. Josh is my responsibility.' Helen started up the stairs before there were any more objections. She had a long way to climb. And she needed to get to the top before anything bad happened to Josh.

* * *

The man unclamped his hand from Josh's mouth.

'No more singing,' he said. 'No more noise.'

Josh nodded, not daring to say anything more. But he'd

197

managed it. Had it been enough? They must have heard him. And he couldn't hear any shouting from down below, so they must have understood his warning. He sat, mute, one arm wrapped around the rail. He wished he could climb back up to the platform above, away from that black hole.

The man went to the other side of the trapdoor and wrenched away more of the wood. Some of it fell into the nave, taking a scarily long time to clatter to the ground. Then with a length of wood, the man knocked the hook until it was swinging back and forward like a pendulum. Josh watched, wondering if he was trying to hypnotise him.

Finally, it came close enough for the man to grab. Strong as he was, Josh could see him stagger slightly under the weight as he braced himself to stop the swing.

'Come here,' he said.

Josh hung onto his railing. He shook his head, mouth clamped shut. There was no way he was going anywhere near the man while he had hold of that hook.

'Don't be stupid.' The man started to work his way around the trapdoor towards Josh, but the heavy hook made him slow.

Josh got to his feet, moved away from him around the circle. The man stopped, switched direction. So did Josh.

He saw frustration in the man's face. He looked really upset, as if he hadn't realised this would happen. Josh had a sudden image of the man as he must have been at school, trying to get his bag back as the other boys tossed it first one way, then another around a mocking circle. The laughter, the taunting. It had happened to Josh a few times, but he'd managed to laugh it off. He remembered the fury, though, the frustration. He almost felt sorry for his abductor.

'Look, I'm just scared,' he said. 'I don't want to get hurt. Tell

198

me what you want to do, then I'll stop.'

The man hesitated, as if trying to decide whether to trust him. 'You won't,' he said, his voice heavy with experience.

'I will. I'll help you. What are you trying to do? What did your mum say?' asked Josh.

The man stared at him, eyes impassive. 'She said I should get rid of you.'

Josh swallowed. 'Why?'

'Because you can identify me. And if I don't do it, she will.'

Josh tried to take in the idea that someone's mum might actually kill him. Some of his schoolfriends' mums didn't like him much. Fin, for example, said it wouldn't be a good idea for Josh to meet his parents.

'She doesn't even know me,' he said.

The man shrugged. 'Makes no difference.'

Josh clung to the railing. 'Please don't,' he said. He could hear his voice shaking. 'I promise I won't tell anyone about you.'

The man gave his secretive smile again. 'I've got an idea. But you have to let me put you on this hook,' he said.

Josh's voice disappeared altogether. He managed a squeak of protest.

'If I tie you to that hook, then lower you into the middle of the cathedral, I can get away. And she won't be able to reach you. They'll find you in the morning and get you down,' he said.

Josh found his voice. Even if it worked, even if the people in the cathedral were already on their way up the steps...

'No,' he whispered. 'I'll fall off. I'd die.'

In reply, the man swung the hook across at Josh. He jumped backwards. The hook swung slowly, too slowly to hit him, but he didn't think it was a good sign.

He grabbed the lowest strut of the railing and swung his leg over. If he could get to the stairs and shut the door at the top and if whoever was coming to find him was already on their way up…

A crushing weight slammed into his side. His lungs felt frozen, the breath knocked out of him. His head cracked against something hard. He gasped, trying to get air back into his lungs. Then an arm gripped around his waist and he was dragged away from the railing. He kicked his feet, trying to loosen his captor's grip.

For a second, he was bewildered, his brain scrambling to catch up with what had happened. Then he realised. The man was standing on the hook, had used it to swing across the trapdoor and grab him. He looked down, saw the black void of the cathedral open up below them. All that was keeping him from falling was the man's grip around his waist.

Josh stopped kicking. A hot trickle of wee ran down his leg. He screwed his eyes tight shut.

'Please,' he whispered. 'Please.'

CHAPTER THIRTY-FOUR

Helen could see light painting the wall of the spiral staircase up ahead.

She stopped, chest heaving from the climb, hands on her knees. She was pouring with sweat, despite the cold night. The top was close now, judging by the light. A turn or two more of the stair. She unlaced her walking boots and slipped them off. She didn't want Josh's captor to hear her coming.

She heard a thump and a stifled gasp. What was happening? She tiptoed up the final few steps to the top of the staircase.

Helen blinked, her eyes adjusting to the light. She couldn't see anyone. A giant wooden treadmill and a beam next to it, from which hung a rope. The rope was swinging from side to side. It disappeared into a gap in the floorboards, surrounded by wooden railings.

Cautiously, Helen approached and looked down.

The man had his back to her, but the sway of the rope could bring him round to face her at any time. She could see Josh's head, his face pressed into the man's shoulder. Beneath his feet, the hook on which the man was balanced. And then the wide semicircle of darkness, opening onto nothing.

A lurch of nausea hit her in the stomach. She gripped the

rail. If the man let go of Josh, he would fall. If he let go of the rope, or stepped off the hook, they would both fall. How was she going to stop that from happening?

Before she could form a plan, the rope turned and they slowly swung around. The man saw her, seemingly without surprise. His dull eyes barely blinked. She tried and failed to see any resemblance between the man and his sparky red headed sister.

'Has my mother sent you?' he asked. 'I need to talk to her.'

Helen thought quickly. 'Jean? She's coming,' she said. 'She wanted me to tell you to keep calm.'

Josh looked up at her voice, twisted his head around to see her. His face was wet with tears and snot. She tried to smile reassuringly.

'I'll just come down here and sit with you,' she said. She paused to see if the man would accept this. He nodded and she climbed carefully down the wooden structure, trying not to think of the gap beneath them.

Helen sat on the bricks around the edge of the hole, one arm wrapped around a railing. The main thing seemed to be to keep them all calm. Sarah Greenley was on the way. She'd know what to do. Trained negotiators. Maybe some sort of safety netting? But time, there was no time. The man couldn't hang on forever, and nor could Josh.

'I'm Helen,' she told him. 'And you're Oliver, aren't you, Jean's son.'

He gave no response.

'And that's Josh with you, my friend Josh,' she said. She was about to tell Josh not to worry when she remembered what he always said about that. And if there was ever a situation which called for worry, this was it. 'I'm going to stay with you

202

Josh,' she said, hoping she sounded more confident than she felt. 'Until Oliver's mother gets here with some help. Then we can all go home.'

'I want Mum.' Josh's voice was muffled against Oliver's shoulder.

'I know you do.' Helen was assessing the distance. The circle was about five foot across. The hook was swinging in the middle, about two and a half feet from the edge where she sat. Too far to reach. She wondered how the pulley system worked; if she could find a way to swing them back to safety. But then she might get it wrong and release the rope, or Oliver might drop Josh as it started to move.

On the far side of the circle, almost half of the trapdoor remained in place. It lessened the gap to less than a foot. But was it strong enough to take her weight? Would it splinter and fall into the void?

She got carefully to her feet and slowly walked around to the other side.

'Stop it,' yelled Oliver. 'Don't do that. Or I'll let go.'

Helen froze.

'No! Ollie, no.' The shriek rose from the depths of the cathedral. Charlie's voice, raw with terror. Oliver shifted his grip and Josh slipped an inch or two. He was whimpering like a mistreated puppy. Helen hardly dared breathe, her heart thudding so hard she could feel it throughout her whole body.

'Who's that?'

Helen took advantage of his shift in attention to move to the broken boards, the splintered semi-circle just beyond the bricks. She knelt down, crept closer to the edge.

'It's me,' called Charlie. 'Ollie, listen to me.'

Helen inched closer.

203

'Why should I?' His voice was sulky, a child refusing to listen to a teacher.

'Because I'm on your side,' said Charlie.

'You're not! You were never on our side,' yelled Oliver. 'You left. You reported us.' He twisted violently, trying to see down past Josh's head.

Helen swallowed hard. Josh had his eyes fixed on her, his mouth stretched into a silent scream. She hooked one foot over the railing and began to crawl onto the broken wood.

'Ollie, I was. I still am. I had to get away from Mum. I was trying to help you. But I'm still your sister.'

'Where's Mum?' shouted Oliver. 'I want Mum. She'll know what to do.'

The wood creaked. Helen felt it bow, very slightly, beneath her knees. She paused, sweat breaking out across her face. No choice. She had to reach the boy. She placed one hand on the broken edge of the door, pressed it gently. It moved, but it might not break.

'Ollie, Mum's no good. You must know that? Why would she make you do these stupid things?'

Helen lay flat across the board. It took her weight. But how much more could it take before it broke?

Oliver looked up, bewildered, and faced Helen. 'You said she was coming,' he said. 'You said we were waiting for her.'

She licked her lips, tried to find a voice in her dry throat. 'That's right. But maybe we could wait here, where it's safe. I could help you get to safety.'

He shook his head. 'You lied.'

Far beneath them, Helen heard a door open. Heels rang out across the stone floor, a long stride. Suddenly, the lights were on below, flooding the nave.

She craned her neck to see what was happening. Two women walked to the base of the tower – Sarah Greenley and a tall woman, blonde, in a long, dark coat.

'No! Don't let her,' Charlie shouted.

The woman called up to the tower.

'Oliver, you stupid child, stop that. You're on your own this time. I'm not going to get you out of trouble again.'

He roared, an anguished wordless sound that echoed around the vaulted ceiling. Then he let go of Josh.

The boy screamed, lurching forward with his arms outstretched. Helen grabbed blindly, her hands suddenly full of fabric. His anorak. Then the shock of the weight of his body, wrenching her hands, her arms. She clung on, felt the wooden boards creak beneath her. The boy's arms were around her neck, a sharp smell of sweat and urine and salt tears.

'It's OK,' she breathed into his dark curls. Was she strong enough to pull him up into the loft? 'Keep holding onto me. I won't let you go.'

'Helen. Lie still. I'm right behind you.' A male voice, reassuring and professional. 'I'm trained in search and rescue. I'm going to clip a line to your belt, then we'll help you bring him slowly up. Can you hold on a moment longer?'

'Yes.' Helen squeezed Josh tight, tears spilling over onto her cheeks.

Sounds of commotion – Sarah Greenley shouting, Charlie yelling – rose from below. Helen looked across at Oliver, who was gazing down at the chaos. He looked utterly wretched, like an abandoned dog left tied to a post for too long. He lifted himself free of the hook, began to haul himself up on the rope, hand over hand.

'Oliver, no,' she called. 'Wait.'

205

It was too late. Helen pressed Josh's face into her shoulder as the man plunged past them. Then all she could hear was the sound of women screaming.

CHAPTER THIRTY-FIVE

Y ou saved the little boy. That's the main thing.' Alice's voice was freighted with sadness.

Helen sipped her tea. Sunlight played on the bunch of yellow chrysanthemums in the blue jug on the table. Outside, autumn sunshine turned the lawn a deep green.

'And you did all you could. William would have known that.' Helen reached out and laid her hand over the bumps of Alice's arthritic knuckles.

'Well,' she said, 'I feel badly about Oliver, too. I should have paid more attention to the children, back in Chatham. But I was always so caught up in my work, and there seemed to be quite enough to do with my own boys.'

'You can't look after everyone,' said Helen. And yet she knew how hard it would have been to live with herself had she not been able to save Josh. Even after the firemen had brought them both safely down to the ground, she'd wanted to keep the boy close to her, feel the warmth of his body, comforting in its smells and sounds and life. If this was just a fraction of what parents felt for their children, she wasn't sure if she could bear the fierceness of that bond.

And Jean Forbes, Oliver's mother. How had she borne it, the destruction of her son in front of her eyes, driven to jump by

her own cruel taunts? Sarah was living with that guilt now
her decision to bring Jean into the cathedral in the hope she
would talk Oliver down. She was trying to put together a case
against the woman, but as Oliver had committed the attacks
it was proving difficult to charge her with murder. The case
relied on Alice's testimony that Jean had been the one directing
operations.

'I never managed to find the epilogue,' Helen said, in an
attempt to distract them both from the horrors of the past few
days. 'I've drawn a blank with that last clue.'

Alice's china-blue eyes brightened. 'And you think the clue
were left by William?'

Helen nodded and pulled the surviving pieces of paper from
her bag. 'Here. Keep them. That's his writing, isn't it?'

The old woman took the scrolls of paper, untied the crimson
silk and smoothed it out.

'It's him,' she said, her voice soft. 'Embroidery silk.'

'How do you know?' She hadn't yet seen the handwriting.

Alice got up and went into her bedroom. When she returned
she was carrying a framed embroidered panel, three foot long
and bright with colour.

'The Canterbury pilgrims,' she said, proudly. 'Look.'

'It's amazing.' Helen leaned over the embroidery, identifying
the figures. The Wife of Bath, with her crimson stockings, her
face merry, leading the pilgrimage. Crimson thread. And there
again, in the Miller's flushed cheeks, the Knight's fluttering
pennant. 'Did you do this?'

Alice laughed. 'I'd never have the patience. It was William.
His hobby, since he was in the army. He was a member of the
Embroiderers' Guild, you know. He made it for my birthday.'

Helen remembered something else. Alice's pendant – now

firmly fastened around her neck again – held a length of crimson thread. She was starting to realise how much the two friends had meant to each other. Love wasn't just for the young, after all.

'Tell me the clue again,' said Alice, briskly. 'I like a puzzle.'

Helen blinked back tears. 'I lost the original. But it was something like, remember the number of the steps. I thought it must be the pilgrim steps in the cathedral.' She'd been back the previous day, walked up the stairs and looked all around them. Nothing. 'Unless you think it could have been the steps to the tower?' Helen certainly wasn't going up those steps again in a hurry. If William had hidden the epilogue in the tower, she thought, it could stay there.

Alice cocked her head to one side, thinking. Then she smiled. 'Thirty-nine,' she said. 'And if I'm right, you'll find out what that means soon enough. When are you going back to London?'

'This afternoon. After I've called into the hospital to see Greg.' Helen brightened at the thought. 'He's recovering really well. I'm taking him some books.' This would be her second visit to the actor. Now she was over her star-struck shyness, she was enjoying his company. Their shared passion for the drama of Shakespeare and Marlowe meant they had plenty to talk about.

'Good for you.' Alice's eyes twinkled, but she didn't tease Helen about him. 'Give me a call when you're home.

* * *

Finally, thought Helen. She paused to shift the rucksack off her shoulder and dug out her keys. The tall Victorian house loomed kindly above her. She pushed through the big black door and paused at the bottom of the stairs, listening as always for the chatter of her neighbour's television from the basement flat.

She shuffled through the pizza delivery leaflets and charity appeals on the shelf where they put the post. A long padded envelope, addressed to her in a familiar small black script. It had been sent recorded delivery, which meant one of the neighbours must have signed for it. She weighed it in her hands and checked the post mark. October 12, the day before she'd left to go to Canterbury. Only a week ago, yet it felt like years.

Sitting on the stairs, Helen slit it open and gently shook the contents out.

She held her breath. Long pages of parchment, covered in faded brown ink, tied with a length of crimson embroidery silk. Secretary hand. Christopher Marlowe's handwriting. The missing epilogue to the play. Wondering, she raised it to her face and inhaled its worn paper smell.

She pulled out her mobile phone. Alice answered immediately.

'He posted it to me,' said Helen. 'I don't understand.'

'Yes, I thought he might have done.' Alice laughed, mischievous sound that told Helen she would be all right, in the end. 'You're too young,' she said. '*The Thirty-Nine Steps* was William's favourite film. It involves a spy on the run, who posts the incriminating documents just before he's assassinated at St Pancras railway station. You'll have to watch it now.'

'I will,' said Helen. 'What should I do with the epilogue?'

'Ah,' said Alice. 'That's rather up to you.'

St Pancras. Helen travelled there frequently, crossing the busy station concourse to the red brick edifice of the British

Library next door. She was on friendly terms with the staff in the library, who had helped in the restoration of the rest of the Marlowe play. The play itself was held in the vaults. Maybe it was time to reunite the epilogue with the manuscript, he thought. Let future scholars make the discovery anew. Keeping the secret had cost enough lives already.

She'd call the library in the morning. She yawned, slipped the envelope into her rucksack and started the long climb up to her fourth-floor flat.

* * *

Enjoyed The Crimson Thread?

If you enjoyed *The Crimson Thread*, please consider leaving a review online. Reviews really help other readers like you to discover my books.

Helen Oddfellow will be back! To follow her continuing adventures, why not sign up to my free readers' newsletter? You'll be the first to know about talks, events, special offers and giveaways. Sign up at annasayburnlane.com.

Notes and acknowledgements

Many of the Canterbury settings for The Crimson Room are real and can be visited. Particularly worth a visit are Canterbury Cathedral, the Marlowe Theatre, Greyfriars Chapel and Eastbridge Hospital, when open. Other places are fictional.

Some of the history – such as the murder of Thomas Becket in Canterbury Cathedral – is real too. However, the plot, people and action of the novel are entirely fictional. There is no play about Thomas Becket by Christopher Marlowe, much as I wish there was. Eastbridge Hospital remains a charitable institution with no hidden secrets that I am aware of.

Thanks are due to Jane Cook, who leant me her research notes about Canterbury Cathedral and courteously answered my nosy questions about volunteering there; to Owen Harmer, sub sacrist at Canterbury Cathedral, and Dr David Flood, former master of choristers at Canterbury Cathedral, who were very helpful in answering questions about the choir and the cathedral. Inaccuracies and liberties taken with the facts are mine alone.

Books consulted:
The Reverend Canon D Ingram Hill: *Canterbury Cathedral*; *Christ's Glorious Church: The story of Canterbury Cathedral*.

About the Author

Anna Sayburn Lane is a writer, editor and journalist. She lives on the Kent coast. Anna has published award-winning short stories and was picked as a Crime in the Spotlight new author at the 2019 Bloody Scotland International Crime Writing Festival. Her 2018 debut novel Unlawful Things was shortlisted for the Virago New Crime Writer award.

You can connect with me on:

- https://annasayburnlane.com
- https://twitter.com/BloomsburyBlue
- https://www.facebook.com/annasayburnlane

Subscribe to my newsletter:

- http://eepurl.com/dyUtmX

Also by Anna Sayburn Lane

Helen Oddfellow never intended to be a sleuth. But she can't let a mystery alone.

As an academic researcher and part-time London tour guide, Helen is equally at home reading in a dusty archive or walking the streets of the capital. Her drive to uncover the truth leads her into some unexpectedly dangerous situations. Uncovering secrets can come at a high cost, when other people want to keep them hidden.

Unlawful Things

A hidden masterpiece. A deadly secret buried for 500 years. And one woman determined to uncover the truth.

When London tour guide Helen Oddfellow meets a historian on the trail of a lost manuscript, she's intrigued by the mystery - and the man. But the pair are not the only ones desperate to find the missing final play by sixteenth century English playwright Christopher Marlowe. What starts as a literary puzzle quickly becomes a quest with deadly consequences.

Unlawful Things was shortlisted for the Virago New Crime Writer award.

"I've never used the word 'masterpiece' in a review before, but Unlawful Things deserves it." – Bookmark That

The Peacock Room

A literary obsession. An angry young man with a gun. And one woman trying to foil his deadly plan.

When Helen Oddfellow starts work as a lecturer in English literature, she's hoping for a quiet life. But trouble knows where to find her.

There's something wrong with her new students. Their unhappiness seems to be linked to their flamboyant former tutor, Professor Petrarch Greenwood. When Helen is asked to take over his course on the Romantic poet William Blake, life and art start to show uncomfortable parallels. Disturbing poison pen letters lead down dark paths, until Helen is the only person standing between a lone gunman and a massacre.

"This is a clever, slow burn of a thriller that builds the tension gradually up to a nail biting end." - Orlando Books.

Printed in Great Britain
by Amazon

64541815R00130